A Touch of Seduction

a novella

An Unlikely Husband
Series: Book 3

by
Mary Campisi

Dedication

To my mother
because you believed—
thank you.

Love and Betrayal...Regency Style

He was the second son of an earl.
She was the daughter of a vicar.
They were young, in love, and believed nothing could keep them apart...
Oh, but they were so very wrong.

Jason Langford fell in love with Ariana Kendrick the first time he saw her. It didn't matter that she was but a vicar's daughter and he was the second son of an earl. Nothing mattered but their love and the future they planned as husband and wife.

But those dreams were torn apart one fall afternoon—swiftly, painfully, tragically.

Nine years later, Jason and Ariana will meet again.

They'll be caught in a tangle of lies, deceit, and intrigue. Where has she been all these years, when Jason thought her dead? Why is she using a name other than her own? Is she truly a widow? When she and her son are rescued walking along a road, why does she have no traveling cases? No carriage? Not even a coat? And the boy she insists is not his son? Is that yet another lie?

It will take great effort to untangle the truth from the lies, but Jason is determined to learn what really happened to the woman he loved, the one he could never forget...and never stopped loving...

An Unlikely Husband Series:

Book One: *The Seduction of Sophie Seacrest* (Sophie & Holt's story)

Book Two: *A Taste of Seduction* (Francie & Alexander's story)

Book Three: *A Touch of Seduction*: a novella (Ariana & Jason's story)

Book Four: *A Scent of Seduction* (Julia & Jon's story)

Print ISBN: 978-1-942158-02-8

Prologue

Nine years earlier

Ariana Kendrick had never been inside a home as grand as Ellswood, but then, she was but a vicar's daughter and her experience of residences other than her own were limited to cottages and the like of fellow parishioners. There had never been a need or an occasion to peer inside an estate of the ton, and certainly not to take tea with an earl, but here she was, waiting for the man to make an appearance. Her gaze fell once again to the magnificence of the drawing room: the massive stone fireplace, the matching striped chairs, the highly glossed table. Did a person ever grow accustomed to the ornate designs of the woodwork or the softness of the Aubusson rugs? And what of the blood-red draperies covering the windows? Even the floors held a certain refined quality about them, as though to signify the wealth and entitlement of its inhabitants.

Jason Langford was raised here, most likely ran in the hallways, bounded down the winding staircase, and stood before the great fireplace in the sitting room. Or did he? Perhaps he was forbidden to play and make childish mischief among such grandeur; perhaps the beauty of the estate was more for visual appeal and not for actual living.

Still, what must Ellswood look like at Christmas? She pictured lights and gaiety and laughter, and at the very center was Jason, the young man who owned her heart. She smoothed her pink day gown and wished she possessed something finer for a meeting with Jason's father. It would not do for her to appear overly common, especially due to the delicate subject matter that she was certain he would broach. What did a man of such wealth and power say to the vicar's daughter who carried his son's baby in her belly?

The possibilities overwhelmed Ariana, suffocated thought and common sense. Oh, but was it too much to hope for a fairy tale outcome? She and Jason loved one another— immensely. Could their love not conquer all manner of difficulty and make the impossible possible? *Yes*, her heart thumped, indeed it could. She leaned against the soft cushions of the sofa and dreamed her happy ending.

A wealthy young man defies class boundaries and falls in love with a woman of common birth. They pledge their love to one another into eternity, and because they are young and believe love does indeed surpass all manner of difficulties, they lie together, sharing their bodies through that pledge. Summer nights are filled with passion and promise, each joining more eager than the last. Until the young man returns to University with a vow to inform his father he wishes to leave school and wed the woman who has stolen his heart. Except the man does not return soon enough, and the young woman finds herself with child.

The choices dwindle as her "state" becomes obvious with the gentle swelling of her belly, a fact she cannot deny. Her father, a vicar with two other daughters, believes one must always own up to one's choices with honor and responsibility. He contacts the young man's father, a nobleman of great authority, who requests a meeting with Ariana to discuss the "situation."

And now, here she sat, on a sofa of such fine quality she could bury her fingers in the cushions and think of nothing but their plumpness. At least that would relax the jumpiness of her belly, a reaction that had nothing to do with the babe and everything to do with meeting Jason's father. She'd seen the man fewer than a handful of times, but his very presence intimidated her: the tall, erect build, the unsmiling expression, the navy eyes. And then there were the tales from the villagers of the man's coldness and lack of compassion; some said it extended to his own family, especially the eldest son who had been shipped off to become a man. Jason did not speak of his father or whether the tales about his brother were mere fabrication on the part of those loving an interesting yarn, or if they were true. Nor did he mention the tragic death of his mother, and Ariana had not possessed the courage to inquire.

There had been a sadness behind his smile; she'd noticed it the first time they met along the path where she gathered lavender for sachets. It was a secret spot, doused with sun to make the lavender grow. Jason had been riding and came upon her in a rush of hoofs and gallops, forcing her from the path. When he spotted her, he stopped, stared for a full three breaths. And then he smiled.

"Miss Kendrick?"

The deep voice roused Ariana from her thoughts of Jason. Edward Langford, the Earl of Westover, stood before her, much taller than he'd seemed from a distance. His expression appeared sterner, his eyes darker. A most formidable presence, one she would rather have avoided. Fear pricked her at the thought of facing this man alone in his son's obvious absence. She stood and curtsied. "Lord Westover."

The man did not speak until he'd had ample time to study her as though she were a prize cow or a roasting hen. Why was he studying her so? Did he believe she had made up the tale of carrying Jason's babe? Or was he attempting to decide whether or not she was suitable to carry a child with Langford blood?

"Sit. Please." His gaze landed on her belly, shifted to her

face. "Would you care for a refreshment?" He pointed to the tea and pastries laid out in front of her. "Our cook makes the best almond cookies in the area." His thin lips pulled into an almost smile. "No one else's can compare."

Ariana nodded and eased an almond cookie onto her plate. To do anything less might appear an insult given the conviction behind his words. "Thank you." She bit into the cookie, chewed, and attempted a smile that failed. She wished he would not stare at her so. Why was the man still standing? Was it an effort to intimidate? Were that his goal, he needn't do anything more than look at her, for his very presence and those eyes were indeed great producers of fear *and* intimidation.

Just as her neck began to ache from looking up at him, he took a seat across from her, leaned forward, and selected an almond cookie from the tray. He popped the cookie in his mouth and chewed with a methodical purpose that spoke of patience and control. "I understand you have two siblings, both younger than you."

"I do." *Of what consequence were her sisters? Moreover, how would he know of their existence unless he'd inquired? And why would the man inquire?*

The earl nodded. "Your mother, does she not have a condition of the lungs that requires her to stay indoors and seek assistance from the neighbors?"

"Yes." *Had Father told him this?* Odd, for he did not like to discuss their mother's condition with anyone except when necessary, and he never expanded the discussion outside of his own parishioners. How then did this man know such a thing? And what else did he know?

"You're a great help as well, are you not? Tending the younger ones, preparing meals and the like?"

Ariana wished she were more skilled in the art of

subterfuge and conversations where one said one thing and meant another. Jason's father had no more interest in her siblings or her ability to help them than a chicken did. And yet, what were his true intentions in regard to such pointed questions? Was he attempting to paint a picture of how unsuitable she was for his son? Jason had vowed they would be together as husband and wife and he did not even know about the baby yet. If this were her penance for marrying outside of her class, she would tolerate it, though she did not like the earl's upper-handed manner. Not one bit. A sliver of anger swirled through her but she held her tongue and forced out a bland response. "I help our family as required. Is that not what family does, Lord Westover?"

His dark gaze narrowed, flitted to the region of her belly once again, and darted back to her face. "Indeed we do, which is why I asked to meet with you today."

Now she would learn the true nature of this meeting and whether he would fight to keep her and Jason apart. *Let him try.* Jason loved her. She carried his child. *Nothing would keep them apart.* The moment he returned home on holiday, she would tell him everything, and they would figure out a plan, one that included a marriage license. She wished her mother had not noticed her growing belly or the stomach upset that forced Ariana to divulge the secret relationship *and* her pregnancy to Jason Langford. Of course, her father had deemed it necessary to contact the earl who appeared determined to ask questions with double meanings, for what purpose she could not say, though she guessed it involved a trap of some sort.

"Would you like to hear my plans?" he asked, invading her thoughts.

No, she wanted to say, *I have no desire to hear your plans. You see, money and title do not make an honorable person, and they certainly do not guarantee happiness.* Instead, she pulled her lips into a smile and said, "I would." Let the man talk, let him go on and on and say whatever he wanted; she and Jason would not fall prey to his demands.

The earl tapped his chin with a long, graceful finger and said in a quiet tone, "You shall finish your confinement at your uncle's in Cornwall. Once the baby is born, you will travel to an acquaintance of mine whose wife has lost several babies. It appears Lady Nightingale is touched in the head with this latest loss and has required confinement of a special nature." He rubbed his jaw and slowed his speech as if formulating the plan as he spoke. "Lord Nightingale says the babes never drew their first breath. Sad business, but one that might have an agreeable solution tied to it, for all parties involved."

"I am very sorry for their loss, but I do not understand what this has to do with me."

"Why, it has everything to do with you, don't you see?" His voice thrummed with conviction. "Margaret needs a child. You are an unwed young woman without means. I think you would both suit." He paused, his dark eyes glittering. "You will give Margaret your child and you may remain as its governess."

"I will do no such thing!" Ariana laid her hands on her belly to dispel the man's horrible words. He could not be serious. One did not *give away* one's child to anyone, irrespective of her situation or the other person's unfortunate plight in life. Could he not see that money and station did not excuse such a request? When she could once again draw a clean breath and speak without a quiver in her voice, she said, "I am indeed sorry for the woman's loss, but you cannot simply *take* my child." Her hands tightened on her belly. "And I am aghast that you would expect you might."

The smile that spread over the earl's face frightened her. "I do not expect, Miss Kendrick. I demand it."

"You must cease such talk at once." Ariana snatched her bonnet from the sofa and stood. "Excuse me, but I must leave." No wonder tales of his harsh ways and disregard for his children swirled about the countryside. Perhaps the death of his wife had left him incapable of sympathy, though there had been too many rumors linking him with dalliances to believe the death of Lady Westover had been more than a passing inconvenience. Ariana thrust her bonnet on her head and made her way to the large oak door, anxious to rid herself of the miserable man Jason called *Father*.

"He won't marry you."

That stopped her. How dare he speak as though he knew how she and Jason felt about one another? She turned and faced him, relieved that several paces separated them. "I believe that is Jason's decision."

He approached her, one calculated step at a time, stopping when he was close enough to reach out and touch her should he desire to do so, which, thankfully, he did not. If he were not such a dreadful man, she might consider him handsome, but the cruelty in his words spoke of an evilness in his heart and a hole that could not be patched. "Jason is but a boy of twenty. And—" his lips curved into a half smile "—he's betrothed to another."

Ariana grew lightheaded, stumbled and caught herself. "That cannot be."

The man's voice gentled. "Jason is indeed betrothed. It was arranged years ago. She's the daughter of an earl and a friend of mine. I am surprised and disappointed my son did not tell you this—" he settled his gaze on her belly "—but it would appear he had his reasons."

She shook her head as seeds of betrayal attempted to take root in her brain. *Jason had lied to her?* No, he would never do that. He loved her; he wanted to marry *her*, not some girl who had been foisted upon him when he was a child. Ariana swiped at her tears and forced out the words she knew to be true. "Jason loves me."

The man lifted a shoulder and sighed. "Many a man loves one woman and marries another. It's the way of things among our society. I have no doubt Jason cares about you; he may even fancy himself in love with you."

She inched toward him, anxious to make him see the truth. "He does love me, and I love him."

But Jason's father had his own truths to share. "More's the pity, because it will change nothing. Jason will marry his betrothed and you will produce a bastard child, admitting him to reduced circumstances and a treacherous life of want. Why would you do that, Miss Kendrick, when I have given you and the child a way out? All you need do is permit a grieving mother to raise the child as her own, while you stand by as governess." His voice dipped to a persuasive rumble. "Do you not think a governess has a greater effect on a child's life and welfare than his mother? A governess cares for the tot, bathes and feeds him, instructs him in his letters and proper comportment. What does a mother do other than provide an occasional hug or pat on the head, and only when it proves convenient for her?"

"That might be the way of the upper crust, but it is not how my family lives."

"Ah." He nodded, a small smile sneaking about his lips. "Quite noble. And messy, I am sure, and not only the nappies, but the emotions. A tiresome lot, I would imagine."

"But a most worthwhile endeavor." What greater joy

than to raise one's own child and instill in him the virtues of honest living?

"Perhaps." Lord Westover checked his timepiece and said, "I have a meeting I must attend. Stay and enjoy the almond cookies, take a few to your sisters if you like. It was a pleasure to meet you, Miss Kendrick. I do see why my son was so taken with you."

Ariana stared at him. "Sir? I told you I will not give up my child."

"That you did. And I informed you that my son is not going to marry you. What I neglected to mention was the other part of the deal. Should you decline to follow my wishes, and it is certainly your choice to do so, I will destroy your father and the rest of your family. What would his parishioners say if they learned his daughter was unwed and with child, that she'd lain with many men and therefore could not name the father?"

"But that is not true!"

"I know that and you do as well, but what about your father's congregation? What will they believe when they are but sinners themselves? To witness their leader in such a state of disgrace will make them more comfortable with their own sins. Yes, I have found people are indeed weak creatures who would rather follow the suggestions of others, even if untrue, than utilize their own mental capacity to reach a conclusion." He laughed, a sinister sound that filled the room. "It is called persuasion and I am very, very good at it."

He would lie and create falsehoods to destroy her family? "But why would you do such a thing?"

His lips thinned and he spat out more evil. "Because I am a businessman."

"You would do this for money?"

"Oh, indeed. Quite a lot of money. Now think on this and let me know your decision in three days. If you agree, your child will want for nothing, neither will your family, and you shall be the child's governess, ever present and recognized in everything but name."

"And Jason?" she ventured, her chest aching. "What of him?"

"You'll never see him again."

Chapter 1

Nine years later

After two long years, Jason Langford had come home! Ellswood bustled with excitement and preparations for a celebration created laughter and anticipation that had never before been felt at the estate. The days of the late Lord Westover had shrouded the inhabitants in angst, disappointment, and long faces save for the few moments of happiness when the earl was not in residence.

The gloom lifted with the return of the eldest son, but the joy did not fill the house until Holt Langford wed Sophie Seacrest and gave her his heart. Gone were the frowns and cold stares from those navy eyes, and in its place was a softening around Holt's mouth, a gentler tone, and a spirit of hope. Months later, they had a child and soon, they would have another.

This is what Jason returned to one fall afternoon amidst the changing of the leaves and the brisk air as he stepped out of his carriage and into the world he had left two years before. America was open and free and much different from England, welcoming anyone seeking opportunity and a better way of life. All that was required was hard work, wagons of it, and if luck climbed on a person's back, he had a chance. Jason had taken such a chance with a shipbuilder in Virginia named Carson Fontaine, and as luck would have it, the man had a daughter, a lovely one with brains, charm, and a suitable disposition. Melanie Fontaine was the reason Jason had come home, and if all went well, he would return to America with a proposal in hand.

Julia would not mind if he took up permanent residence across the ocean as long as she could accompany him. Of course, she would have a list of expectations and wishes and he was fairly certain he would not agree with any of them. He dreaded the new "tricks" his sister had learned from that wild child Francie Bishop, but there would be several, of that he had no doubt.

Julia in America was not a thought he cared to contemplate. She could not venture there unless it was for a very limited time, and under the careful supervision of a chaperone, preferably not him! He pictured his sister sporting not only his breeches, but his riding boots, lawn shirt, and mayhap even his jacket. No doubt she would wish to learn the workings of a rifle, too. Melanie Fontaine had no desire for such unladylike behavior and that made her all the more attractive to him. A woman should act like a woman and she should certainly dress like one.

Of course, Julia would disagree. Oh, yes, his younger sister subscribed to the wild and free antics of Francie Bishop and by now, she might well have pulled their half-sister, Caroline, under her spell and introduced her to breeches and tramping barefoot on the front grounds. *Egad*, Holt would not have permitted that. Would he? The poor chap was outnumbered by females, and perhaps they had worn him down, bit by bit, day by day, until there was nothing left but to agree to their demands. Jason sighed. Even the strongest of men could be brought down by a band of women in possession of an idea and a plan.

Thankfully, Melanie appeared satisfied to stand by his side—with her shoes and stockings *on*, in a dress, and without a four-legged animal climbing about sofas and chairs. Thankfully, indeed, Melanie Fontaine was nothing like Francie Bishop, in behavior or looks. The latter was as important as the first, for Francie's red hair and blue eyes reminded him of a woman from his past, the one he had loved and lost.

"Sebastian Trent is smitten with Francie and Alexander Bishop's governess." Julia's smile spread as she regaled the details. "There are wagers he will offer for her before the first snowfall."

"Julia." Holt shot her a warning look, which, of course, she ignored.

"Why can I not tell Jason what he has been missing? Sebastian is his friend and he shall hear it from him soon enough."

"She does have a point." This from Sophie who glanced from her husband to Julia before adding, "It might be better if Jason were prepared for the lovestruck condition he'll find his friend in, rather than surprise him with it."

Holt pierced a piece of roast pork and mumbled, "Idiocy."

"Excuse me?" Sophie laid a hand on her husband's arm and raised a brow. "What did you say?"

The faintest splotch of red crept up his neck, spread to his cheeks. Holt Langford, the Earl of Westover, the man who did not like to reveal his thoughts or his feelings, had blushed. This was the true sign of his brother's capitulation into the murky waters of love. Jason could not resist the temptation and offered a response. "I believe my brother said you are his queen and he is your most loyal subject."

Holt narrowed his gaze on Jason and frowned. "I believe I did not."

Julia's laughter spilled over them. "But I think you did say that, Brother. What do you think, Caroline? Did you not hear Holt say Sophie was his queen?"

Caroline giggled and blurted out, "Sophie is Holt's queen and he is her king."

"A king." Holt slid a glance at his wife. "I believe I like

the sound of that."

"Hmm," Sophie said. "No doubt you do."

"Enough talk of kings and queens," Jason said, wondering when his brother had turned as soft as the stuffing from a toy. Maybe that happened when a person was in love. He would not know, nor did he plan to find out. While he cared about Melanie Fontaine and believed she would make a suitable wife and mother of his children, he did not love her, did not plan to love her. That was an emotion he had succumbed to only once in regard to a woman, and the results had been disastrous. There would be no repetition.

"Her name is Ana," Julia said. "I quite like her."

Jason glanced at Caroline and said in a soft voice, "A lovely name. Almost as lovely as Caroline."

The child beamed, her navy eyes shimmering. From the day they learned she was their half-sister, they had welcomed her into their home, teaching her how to speak once again, and also what it meant to be loved. In the two years Jason had been gone, Caroline had bloomed into a lovely young woman, filled with grace and confidence. The loss of her Aunt Vivian from a fever had been the last tie to a childhood marked by ridicule, harsh words, and torment.

"Ana is very pretty," Caroline said. "Kind, too. She has a boy named William. He is very good at chess."

"I see." What he did not see was why his good friend, Sebastian Trent, the future Earl of Barclay, was falling for a woman well below his station, and possibly contemplating marriage to her. *A governess?* Good Lord, why? Even if she were the most beautiful and agreeable woman Sebastian had ever had occasion to meet, that was not a reason to offer marriage. If he simply could not do without her, he should set her up in a townhouse with the child, pay her an allowance, and visit whenever the mood or the need struck him.

"We like her very much. She was rather quiet when she first arrived, but a little time with Francie, and the quietness dissolved." Sophie hid a smile, as though there were specifics to the "dissolving" of the woman's quietness that she preferred not to share.

Jason need not wonder about Francie Bishop's part in stealing the woman's quietness; she probably stole her sanity as well. He picked up a roll and slathered butter on it. Sebastian was too nice, too trusting, and too wealthy. That made him the perfect target for a female with an aim for advancement, namely in the areas of wealth and title. But Sebastian was not blameless either. He longed to rescue every female from her dire situation, real or imagined, and as a result, once he had saved her, he fancied himself in love. This woman would be no different.

One of these days, Sebastian would decide to employ reason instead of emotion and then, he would select a proper wife. But not until then. "Will someone tell me this woman's story? I've accepted a dinner invitation at Sebastian's tomorrow evening and would prefer a bit of information beforehand."

"The usual." Julia rolled her eyes. "Sebastian fancies himself in love again." She paused a few seconds and when she spoke again her voice turned gentle. "But there is something about the way he watches her, as though he cannot quite draw a full breath. His expression turns soft, his mouth parts just so...and his eyes...they shimmer."

"Shimmer?" Holt shook his head. "Are we talking about a gown or Sebastian Trent?"

"You know what I mean. I have seen you look at Sophie that way." She nodded and raised a brow. "And do not try to deny it."

"Maybe his eyes glisten, too," Jason said. "What do you think, Holt?"

Holt's lips twitched. "Shimmer. Glisten. Sparkle?"

Jason laughed. "Shine?"

"Oh, make fun of my observations," Julia said, tossing her napkin on the table and turning to Jason. "You shall see what I am talking about, and then you will not think it funny."

"Julia." Jason hid a smile. "My little sister is so worldly that of course she would notice true love when she spotted it." He slid a glance at Holt, who was doing his damnedest not to laugh. "I appreciate the comments and will observe Sebastian's eyes closely for signs of shimmering."

Julia swatted his arm. "You are horrible." She shot a glance at Holt. "You, too. I have no idea how I tolerate either of you."

"Because of our glistening eyes?" Jason asked.

"Shiny eyes," Holt corrected.

"Ah. Indeed. Shiny eyes." Jason met his sister's gaze and they both burst out laughing.

"I am so happy to have you home again," Julia said. "Look at us—" She waved a hand around the table. "We are a family. All of us; is it not the most wonderful feeling?"

Yes, after all the years of turmoil and uncertainty, it was indeed wonderful. Holt and Sophie were happy, working to expand their family. Caroline was safe and flourishing despite her earlier sadness, and Julia was still the same Julia: independent, opinionated, in need of the right man to show her that life need not be a constant battle for the sake of battle, that joy could be found, and perhaps a modicum of solace. One day, Julia would find such a man and then, perhaps her eyes would be the ones that shimmered.

***

"I have asked her to be my wife." Sebastian Trent, the future Earl of Barclay, smiled and said with what Jason Langford could only signify as a lovesick declaration, "As soon as she will have me."

Not that Jason had ever made many such declarations, perhaps only one and long ago, but the desperation in such a proclamation was easily recognizable and equally pitiable. A man lost to such declarations was well and truly lost. Friends might try to persuade or dissuade, depending on the situation and circumstance, but if a man fancied himself in need of a particular woman's "love," there was no help for that.

And that is exactly what Jason Langford feared in regard to his longtime friend as they sat in Sebastian's library awaiting the arrival of the man's future wife. With his looks, status, education, and genuine likeability, Sebastian Trent could pick any woman on the continent for a wife: young, old, blond, brunette. All he need do was cast a glance at a woman and she practically swooned. Whether the swoon had more to do with Sebastian's future earldom or his dashing good looks, no one knew, though many a mother announced the combination as intoxicating. Why then would such a man select a widow he had known less than four months who possessed a mysterious past and a young son?

It made no sense, unless one fancied himself in love.

"I proposed last evening and Ana accepted. I cannot wait for you to meet her." Sebastian's expression softened to match his voice as he expounded on the virtues of the mysterious Ana. "When she enters a room, she captivates those in attendance without uttering a word. A simple look draws them to her." His voice dipped lower, turned softer.

"Of course she is beautiful, but it is more than that. There is something about the way she holds herself that marks her a woman of esteemed quality who has obviously been raised among the privileged, and yet is not affected by it." He laughed and toyed with his glass of whisky. "I daresay most of our friends are overrun with self-importance, but not Ana." He sighed and a ridiculous smile slipped across his lips, the sign of a truly besotted man. "'Tis quite refreshing, actually."

"Hmm." Jason studied his friend, counting the seconds before he could begin the barrage of direct questions in regard to the woman Sebastian considered a paragon of virtue. How would such a woman find herself on a country road without benefit of carriage or traveling cases and carting along a young son? Oh, Jason had heard the tale of the earl who pressed advances on the family's governess mere weeks after his wife's funeral, forcing the woman to flee the residence with her child. Julia had regaled him with that story too many times and he had only been back two days. But something in that tale reeked like spoiled cabbage. The woman could bring no one into her confidence in order to elicit help for herself, or even her son? Not a single member of the staff, or a "friend"? That bore thinking on and the more Jason tinkered with the idea, the more he disliked what emerged. And yet, how to make Sebastian see that perhaps he had been too trusting, too blinded by the woman's sad tale and young son to recognize the falsehoods behind the words?

"Alexander Bishop found Ana and her son, is that not correct?" Bishop was no milquetoast prone to a soft heart and softer head when it came to reasoning out a situation. There was much to be said about searching for answers in the details, and Bishop was a man of detail and observation.

Yes, Bishop was the key and Jason would find a way to have a word with him in private tonight, perhaps when the others were caught up in Ana's beauty and virtue.

"Yes, Alexander rescued her and William and not a moment too soon either." Sebastian's eyes glittered with emotion. "He found them at dusk, their clothing grimy, shoes muddied, faces coated with fear. I daresay, it was a sign from above that landed them with the Bishops." His smiled stretched. "You know Francie; people and animals in need of help are her specialty."

"Oh, I know Francie." Two years in America had not lessened Jason's agitation when that woman's name was mentioned. Francie Bishop might be a wife and mother, and she might well travel in the same social circles as Jason, but the woman was a wild spirit who cavorted in men's breeches and permitted animals in the house. Possibly even on her bed. Who knew what Francie Bishop might do? Could Alexander Bishop *not* control his own wife?

"Francie considers Ana and William's arrival a godsend and I daresay, I agree."

"Oh? What have the woman and child provided to render such a comment?" Were they all hoodwinked? Surely, Bishop did not agree with his wife's sentiment.

"Ana is a most excellent governess, according to Francie." Sebastian leaned forward and spoke in a conspiratorial manner. "And while Francie insisted she had no need of a governess, once Ana displayed her skills with the children, well, that was that."

A person could be anyone if the stakes were high enough. Had he not seen this with his own brother when Holt returned to Ellswood as Gregory Thurston? And what of Jason's two-year stay in America, during which time he had met any manner of men and women who claimed to possess wealth, titles, even honor, until closer inspection revealed the statements to be false or lacking? People fabricated tales to aid their situation, and while Sebastian's future bride might well be trustworthy and honest with a commendable work history and a spotless past, she might have a blemish or two. Or twelve. He owed it to his longtime and often gullible friend to find out.

"Another whisky?" When Jason nodded, Sebastian refilled their glasses, took a long drink, and sighed. "Can you not be happy for me without attempting to poke holes in my newfound bliss?"

"I am not. I mean, I am happy for you, that is." But his friend had known him too many years, from the time they were seven and riding ponies together, and a person did not simply shed his habits or his attitude like a snake shedding its skin. While Sebastian had grown up in a household filled with love and much laughter, Jason had not. He had coped with the aloofness of his father, the "death" of his mother, the departure of his brother, leaving only his youngest sister to offer an escape from the bleakness of his life. Then he had met Ariana Kendrick, the young woman who had stolen his heart and crushed it, all in the span of a summer.

"I had half thought you might return with a bride."

That comment brought Jason around, quickly. "What? Why would you say that?" Thoughts of Melanie Fontaine suffocated his brain, doused his senses with her lilac perfume and southern drawl. He had partnered with her father seven months ago, entered an agreement that involved the growth of the man's shipbuilding business and provided an introduction to Carson Fontaine's oldest daughter, Melanie, a dark-haired beauty with hazel eyes, a quick wit, and a list of suitors from Virginia to South Carolina. Not that he had been looking for a wife, but

Melanie was no ordinary woman. She played the pianoforte, spoke French, Italian, *and* Latin, wrote poetry, painted vases, engaged in witty and entertaining conversation, and had declined four offers of marriage in the last three months, claiming she wanted no one but Jason.

That was what had brought about the trip home to England. Holt and Julia believed the visit to America was not permanent and while it might be a bit drawn out, they anticipated his eventual return. If he were to offer for Melanie, he would make his home in America. Such news should be delivered in person and until he spoke to his brother and sister, he would not divulge his plans to anyone, not even Sebastian.

"Are you blushing?" Sebastian's gaze traveled from Jason's neck to his face, settled on his cheeks. "I'll be damned, I believe you are."

"Your obsession with your future bride has addled your brain *and* affected your eyesight." Jason shook his head and muttered, "Blushing. What nonsense."

"Out with it. Who is she?"

Damn, but the man was persistent. That trait had marked Sebastian a successful businessman who knew how to make his own money instead of depending on the family fortune like many of his peers did. "Who is who?" Jason possessed patience equal to Sebastian's persistence. He sipped his whisky and rubbed his jaw. Sebastian Trent might be his good friend, possibly his best friend, but Holt and Julia were family, and until Jason spoke with them about taking a bride and remaining in America, he would tell no one else.

Fortunately, a knock on the library door halted any further interrogation. "Come in."

The door opened and Nance, the ancient butler, shuffled in. The man had been old when Jason was a child, but now he appeared as though he had passed from this earth and returned, a whisper of a man composed of wrinkles and gray hair. The wrinkles multiplied when he spoke. "Your guests have arrived."

"Excellent." Sebastian smiled at the man who had served his father until five years ago, when Nance could no longer keep up with the activities in London. That's when Sebastian offered him employment at his estate in the country. The pace was slower and more suitable to a person with creaking bones and slowing steps. "Make them comfortable in the drawing room and see to refreshments. We shall join them directly."

When the butler had shuffled his way out of the room, Jason said, "Can you not retire him? The man can barely walk."

"No." Sebastian finished off his drink and set it on the table. "If I were to let him go, he would be dead within the week. This job gives him purpose and I will not take it away from him."

Jason was still thinking about that when they entered the drawing room. *Everyone must have a purpose*; had not Julia made that statement with heartfelt conviction every time she begged him to let her engage in one pursuit or another, each equally unsuitable for a woman, each encouraged by Francie Bishop? The thought of that woman pinched his right temple until he squinted in pain.

"Jason! How wonderful to see you!" The source of his pain descended upon him in a rush of excitement and threw her arms about him, her over-large belly hindering her attempts to draw him closer. The scene was beyond awkward, but apparently not for Francie Bishop, who acted as though all pregnant women bounced their bellies against men who were not their husband. Thankfully, Alexander

Bishop interceded.

"Francie, I do believe you are embarrassing Mr. Langford."

"I am?" Francie released him and stepped back to consider her husband's comment. "Jason, have I embarrassed you?"

What did a gentleman say to a woman who asked such a pointed question, knowing full well he will hurt her feelings should he tell the truth? Drat, but she left him no choice. He forced a smile and said, "Of course not, Francie." The smile stretched. "Wonderful to see you."

Her blue eyes sparkled and if he set aside the annoyance her free-spirited ways caused him, he could acknowledge her beauty, perhaps even admit she could prove entertaining and endearing. But if he did that, he might find himself spending more time in her company, and that would only permit him opportunity to study the fiery hair, the blue eyes, even the bright smiles that reminded him of Ariana—the woman he had loved and lost so many years ago. Better to avoid Bishop's wife and in so doing, avoid the pain that squeezed his chest with memories of Ariana. It was a coward's way; he recognized that, even acknowledged it. Traveling across an ocean had not erased the pain, but maybe Melanie Fontaine could, for she was the first woman since Ariana who stirred an emotion close to fondness in him.

Francie linked her arm through her husband's and smiled up at him. Bishop was not one for smiles or soft expressions, not with those silver eyes and a scar slashing part of his face, but damn if his wife could not pull the smile and the softness from him.

Sebastian cleared his throat and said in an anxious voice, "Where is Ana?"

"Tending the child," Bishop said, beating his wife to an explanation, though whether such evasive words could be termed an "explanation" proved doubtful.

His wife must have agreed and saw fit to interject and expand as only Francie Bishop could. "Ana will arrive soon. She had to see to William; the poor boy finds it difficult to settle in at night." She paused, her brows furrowed, and added in a low voice, "Bad dreams, I believe."

Jason shot a look at Alexander Bishop who merely shrugged, but the tenseness in his stance indicated there was more to this story than a bad dream or two. Before the night ended, Jason would learn of Bishop's suspicions and perhaps even add a few of his own.

"Who could blame the boy? If I lost my father and were forced to leave my home with nothing but the clothes I wore and threats on my head, I should have bad dreams as well." Sebastian's face lit up and his voice softened when next he spoke. "Whatever those fears, they are over now. No harm will come to Ana or William while under our protection." He nodded at Bishop. "Soon I hope to see to their welfare and their happiness—" his lips spread into a wide smile "—Ana has agreed to marry me."

Francie clapped her hands and let out a squeal that Jason imagined resembled that of the baby pig he'd heard she recently adopted. "I knew it! I absolutely, positively knew you and Ana would suit." She leaned on tiptoe and kissed her husband's cheek with a loud smack, right in the center of the man's scar. Alexander Bishop's lips twitched but his expression remained unreadable, except to Francie, who grasped his arm and smiled up at him. "I'm growing quite adept at this matchmaking business, am I not, Alexander?"

"You are improving, Francie."

She turned to Jason. "Indeed I am. I matched up your

brother long before he knew Sophie would make the perfect wife."

Jason cleared his throat and said, "I would prefer not to remember those days." He had no desire to think about the hurt and anguish Holt and Sophie suffered or his mother's part in it. Past was past and they had found their happiness in each other, and their children. Maybe one day, he would do the same, and maybe that day was waiting for him in America—with Melanie Fontaine.

"I had such hopes of matching you, but alas, you headed to America before I could consider the possibilities. However, now that you have returned, I am certain I could select a few names for your consideration." She slid him a smile and nodded. "I am getting quite good at it."

"No," Jason blurted out, drawing an actual smile from Bishop and a laugh from Sebastian. "I mean, no, but thank you, Francie." When her mouth pulled into a frown and her shoulders sagged, he added, "Truly." And then, because he could have sworn she sniffed, he said, "But I will keep you in mind. In the future." More frowning and shoulder sagging. "The near future."

That seemed to please her. She straightened her shoulders and offered a cautious smile. "May I draw up a prospective list? For the near future consideration?"

He could not tolerate a sad woman. "You may." Bishop cast him a look that said he was an idiot for falling for his wife's antics, but Jason would bet the man had succumbed to them a time or two himself.

"I shall begin the list posthaste and see if we might find the perfect match for you." She tapped her chin and added, "There is a special someone for everyone."

"Francie." Alexander Bishop raised a brow and said, "Near future does not mean posthaste."

She scrunched her nose and stared at her husband. "What? Of course not. I do know the difference between near future and posthaste," she said, as though miffed that he might think her of inferior intelligence. "However, one must be prepared for the time when near future becomes posthaste, as in a business deal, so one does not lose the edge or the opportunity." She settled her hands on her expanding middle and smiled at her business-genius husband. "Is that not correct?"

Alexander sighed. "I believe it is."

If she had not been discussing a potential wife candidate for him, Jason might have enjoyed the sparring between Francie and Alexander Bishop. But the woman's overzealous determination to find him a match outweighed witnessing the couple bandy about insinuations and forced Jason to speak. "I do appreciate your interest, Francie, and fear not, you shall be the first to know when near future becomes posthaste."

That comment brought a tinkle of laughter, followed by a question that told him Francie Bishop did not know the meaning of near future. "Do you have a fondness for blonds, brunettes, or redheads?"

The ancient butler saved him from an answer when he opened the drawing room doors and ushered a woman into the room. Jason caught a swirl of lavender before he turned to study Sebastian's response. *Lovestruck. Absorbed. Enchanted.* The man really did fancy himself in love with her. And what of his counterpart? Would her expression contain equal rapture? Jason shifted his gaze to the woman who had stolen his friend's heart. And froze.

Chapter 2

Ariana spotted Jason Langford three breaths before he saw her, time enough to hide the shock of seeing him again. Nine years was a lifetime ago, one she would rather forget. *One she must forget.* She knew the exact moment he recognized her as evidenced by the sudden paleness of his tanned face, the rigidness of his strong body, the brightness of his gray eyes. He stared, piercing her with a gaze that had once heated her body and made her burn for him.

"At last, two of my favorite people shall meet." Sebastian held out a hand and grasped hers, his smile covering her with admiration. "Ana, this is my good friend, Jason Langford." He turned to his *good friend* and said, "May I present Mrs. Ana Kendall?" And then, as though he could not restrain from a further comment, added, "I told you she was a beauty, did I not?"

Dear Sebastian. In the few short months she had known him, he had proven kind, considerate, and ever attentive, a true gentleman with a big heart and an even bigger desire to see her and William settled and happy. He had vowed to protect them from all manner of fears, including the ones she had fabricated.

"Indeed she is." Jason paused, held her gaze, and bowed. "A true beauty."

His voice no longer held the soft hesitancy of a young man but had turned deep and rich, capable of commanding, or charming, or perhaps seducing. She sucked in a breath of air, prayed for calmness. Had she not pretended for years? What was one more night of play-acting? *Do not let him see he has affected you.*

"Sebastian says you have a son?"

She swallowed, fought down the urge to run from that

inquisitive look, and said in her most nonchalant manner, "I do. His name is William."

"Ah. William. How old is the boy?"

"Eight," she replied, subtracting a year from William's age.

"Eight?" Francie's brows furrowed. "I thought him nine."

"No," Ariana said quickly, perhaps a bit too quickly if Alexander Bishop's intent gaze were any indication. The man was a magician with numbers and memorization. He would not forget William's age.

"I shall look forward to meeting your son—" Jason Langford paused long enough to make her wonder at his next words "—Mrs. Kendall."

She glanced at Sebastian who had the look of a man determined to believe whatever she told him, even if some of the tales were stuffed with untruths. Thinking oneself in love could render a person incapable of logical thought and unwilling to consider anything but the brightest of outcomes.

Oh, but such foolishness came with a harsh lesson that, once learned, would not be repeated.

"I prefer to call Mrs. Kendall Ana. May we please dispense with the formalities?" Francie looked at the group and shrugged. "It sounds so stuffy and I have no tolerance for such, do I, Alexander?"

"No, dear, indeed you do not."

Ariana was quite fond of Francie, despite her free-spiritedness and stable of animals, indoors and out. The woman loved her children, her animals, nature, and most especially, her husband. Alexander Bishop did not seem the type bent to professions of love or strings of sonnets, and yet if one observed the man in the presence of his wife, it soon became obvious he loved Francie—immensely.

Sebastian extended an arm to Ariana and nodded toward the group. "Mrs. Smith prepared cherry tarts especially for you, Francie."

"Delightful! I could almost skip the other courses and head directly to the cherry tarts." She smiled and laid a hand on her stomach. "But I shall restrain. My husband says I must practice restraint more often, especially in regard to my interest in others." She made a face and laughed. "Why on earth would I do that?" Her gaze moved from Sebastian, to Ariana, and landed on Jason, who merely shrugged. "Exactly. There is much to be learned from not only watching others, but listening to them and engaging in casual conversation." Her voice dipped. "My husband does not agree."

Alexander leaned toward his wife and said in a quiet voice, "Your husband has obtained the recipe for Mrs. Smith's cherry tarts."

"Alexander, you are too good to me." She rose on tiptoe and kissed him straight on the mouth. "Thank you."

He nodded, his voice serious, his eyes glittering. "A husband does what he can to keep his wife satisfied."

If not for Francie Bishop's entertaining nature and lively conversation during dinner, Jason Langford might have found an opportunity to pry open Ariana's story and look for the holes. He remained polite but ever watchful, his strong jaw set, his eyes narrowed, as though considering a plan of action. She remembered that about him, how he had been a thinker, exploring possibilities, and he had explored every bit of her one long, hot summer. Goodness, where had *that* come from? Had she not spent years forgetting the man and his touch, remembering instead the lies, the destruction, the pain of losing her family? She chewed a bit of roast, swallowed. The man had not suffered as she had. How could he have when he had been the one telling the lies, causing her such misery? Hiding the fact that he had a betrothed who must be his wife by now. Had they children as well? A girl and a boy with golden hair and sparkling eyes...

"Ana, where is your home?"

Ariana looked up from her plate and stared at Jason Langford. If they were alone, she would lunge across the table and pummel his chest. He knew very well where her home was, or had been. Was he toying with her, seeing what she might or might not say, all in the name of a grand and sick game in which he apparently found humor? Well, she would have none of it. She forced a smile and said, "My home is where my son is, whether that be in a field, a mansion, or a barn."

"How very true," Francie Bishop agreed. "Family is the cornerstone of all dwellings, be they made of straw or brick." She slid a smile at her husband and said, "Is that not true, darling?"

Alexander Bishop nodded, a splotch of red covering his cheeks. "Quite true, Francie. Quite true indeed."

The man might blush at his wife's endearments, but the gentleness in his voice and the brightness in his eyes told a different tale, and that tale said, *Slather me with all manner of endearments, great and small.* The man loved his wife; how utterly refreshing. Ariana would have guessed him to be one not given to emotion or heartfelt words, but according to Francie, her husband was "softer than dough" and just as malleable. Doubtful the man would like knowing his wife compared him to dough, but even so, it would not change his feelings and would most likely elicit no more than a raised brow.

"While I do agree that home is where our loved ones reside, I would hope one might claim a constant location in which to create memories with those loved ones," Sebastian said, his gaze settling on Ariana.

It was her turn to blush, knowing everyone watched her, especially Jason Langford. Had he not once pledged his life *and* his love to her? Did he recall that pledge, or had it been no more than a string of words spoken to bed her, words that had been long forgotten? A sharp twinge worked its way from her belly to her chest. Why did the sight and memories of the man disturb her so? Why could she not look upon him and his lies as one would a forged painting?

"Well spoken," Jason Langford said, his gaze landing on her a second too long.

Why did the man act as though she had offended *him* when he had been the one harboring secrets and withholding truths? They had spent a summer of physical and emotional exploration, speaking of love and marriage, planning to break past class boundaries and unite their families. Jason had been fearless and so certain he would marry her that she believed him and, therefore, she had given herself to him— openly, willingly, with love.

But he had lied.

"Have you a family, Mr. Langford?" The question slipped out before she could pull it back.

He picked up a roll, tore it in half, studied it. "A brother and two sisters." He looked up, a tight smile on his handsome face, and asked, "Do nephews and nieces count? I've one of each and another on the way."

"I see." *And your wife, what about her?* "I may be mistaken," she lied, "but I thought Sebastian mentioned a wife?"

The smile turned brittle, cracked. "Not mine, though I

have had one or two apply for the position."

It was Ariana's turn to tear her roll in half. His words made no sense. Edward Langford had taken great pleasure informing her of his son's betrothal to another. Indeed he had, stuffing implications that the man whose baby she carried had never had any intention of marrying her, despite the sweet words he might have used to seduce her. "Excuse me, Mr. Langford, but were you ever married?"

"No." The force of that single word left no mistake he spoke the truth. "Though I did come close once." He held her gaze, forcing the air from her brain until she could not think. But those eyes, oh they pierced her with anger and something close to despair, stripping her of logic and common sense.

"I have never been married either," Sebastian said in an obvious attempt to lighten the mood swirling about the table. "Though I plan to remedy that soon."

***

Jason waited until the Bishops and Ariana were taking their leave before he pulled Alexander aside and said, "I must speak with you at once about a private matter. May I follow you to your residence?"

Alexander Bishop studied him as though he were a set of numbers that did not quite add up. When Jason thought the man would refuse, Bishop nodded and said, "Very well, though I must see Francie to bed first or she'll pull up a chair and begin her own interrogation."

Of that, Jason had no doubt. "Thank you."

"Give me a quarter of an hour and I shall tell James to expect you." He paused, his silver gaze narrowing, and said, "Do you require Mrs. Kendall's presence?"

Now why would he ask such a question unless he suspected something was amiss? "That will not be necessary." Once he questioned Bishop, he would formulate a plan to get Ariana alone and then he would demand to know why she had disappeared for nine years only to return under an assumed name with a son and a make-believe story.

Jason waited for the allotted time before he entered the home of Alexander and Francie Bishop. He had avoided Francie as much as possible in the past, and while he claimed her free-spirited ways were the reason, that was not exactly true. He had avoided the woman because she bore a painful resemblance to Ariana. The red curls, the sky-blue eyes, on occasion even the tinkling laughter had all reminded him of the woman he had loved and tragically lost. There had not been a grave to visit, or a family member to speak with in regard to details of Ariana's passing. Had she suffered? Had she called his name at the last? What could he ask without rousing suspicion? Nothing at all, and so he had carried the burden of his love and loss for years.

But tonight he learned that Ariana Kendrick was alive and more beautiful than he remembered.

"You look like you could use a whisky." Alexander Bishop entered the room looking as starched and unrumpled as he had hours ago.

"That's the best idea I've heard tonight."

Who would believe that Bishop had once tried to boot Francie from Drakemoor, claiming she was *not* Lord Montrose's long-lost daughter, though she proclaimed to be his child. Lord Montrose had but to take one look at Francie to know his blood ran through her veins. Word had it the old man enjoyed playing matchmaker for Alexander, his surrogate son, and Francie, his daughter. Apparently, Bishop tried to deny the attraction, but he must have failed, because here he was, wed to Francie, father to two with another on the way, and not one bit unhappy about it.

Oh, but Jason would love to hear the details of that story, but he doubted Bishop would share them. He would have to settle for a drink or two and perhaps a bit of information regarding their governess.

Alexander handed him a drink and said, "I expected to hear from you, but I must admit, I thought you would give it a day or two." He paused, eyed him with an astuteness that made Jason look away, and asked, "How may I help you?"

"Your governess, Mrs. Kendall, I'm curious as to how she came to be in your employ."

"Did Sebastian not tell you I found Mrs. Kendall and her son along the road, without a wrap or valise, not even a satchel?"

Jason met his gaze, held it. "I had heard that, but it strikes me as odd, and there are more holes in the story than French lace."

Bishop's lips twitched. "I take it you do not believe the tale?"

"Do you?"

"Not entirely, and less since I witnessed you and Mrs. Kendall together. I daresay, you recognized her and she recognized you."

How had the blasted man deduced *that*? "She resembles your wife, do you not think so?"

Bishop rubbed his jaw, considered this. "No, absolutely not. There is only one Francie."

Thank God for that. "My mistake."

Bishop finished his drink and pointed to a set of high-backed chairs done in a maroon and cream stripe. "Let us sit and formulate possibilities on how and why Mrs. Kendall had occasion to travel as she did when I found her."

What he meant was that he knew Ariana had fabricated a

story and he also knew Jason suspected the same. What he wanted to ponder was why had she done it. Well, Jason had the same question and maybe together, they could hypothesize and reach a conclusion or two. "I'm curious about the man who pressed his advances."

"Ah, yes, the mysterious earl who cannot be found."

"What do you mean? Do you have a name or a location of residence?" Bishop might not be a member of the ton but he did business with enough of them to obtain whatever information he required. Most were keen to stay in his graces and on his ledger as a client for it was well known that Alexander Bishop could make money.

"Not exactly. Ana has always been a bit reticent to speak of her time with her previous employer." He nodded, his dark brows furrowed in thought. "She did mention a Reginald Sumner, but I have not been able to locate the man and my sources have tried."

Because there is no Reginald Sumner, just as there is no story about an earl pressing his advances on her. It was all a ruse, but for what purpose? What had Ariana been doing these past nine years and why was she running from it? That was the real question, the one that would answer all the others. "Do you believe there is a man by that name? Or rather, do you believe there is an *earl* by that name who had an association with Ana?"

Bishop tapped his fingers on the arm of his chair and said, "That is the question, is it not? Of course, Francie wishes to believe Ana and William were the victims of a most dire situation that necessitated the use of cunning and skill to escape." He blew out a long breath, muttered, "My wife is quite the storyteller."

"You do not believe it?"

He shrugged. "I believe there are bits of truth sprinkled

in with the tale, but whether or not that constitutes an accurate story is questionable." He slid Jason a look and said, "I find it interesting that William hesitates at times before he addresses Ana as Mother, and when you asked his age tonight, she stated eight but had told us nine. The question is why?"

Jason stared at his drink, forced his expression to remain blank. Why would Ariana subtract a year from the boy's age unless it was not to her benefit for him to be a year older?

"I also found it odd that the first time Ana heard the Langford name, she turned the color of our cook's flour and practically toppled over. When Sophie Langford extended an invitation to tea, the woman took to her bed with a severe headache. Of course, Francie persisted, and eight days later, she accompanied Ana and William to tea at Ellswood. I heard it was an interesting event, though Ana uttered no more than ten words, claiming a sore throat. Francie found this odd as the woman had perfect command of her speech that very morning, yet lost it the second she crossed the Langfords' threshold."

"Interesting." *The less she said, the fewer lies to keep straight.*

"I hear your name came up that day."

"Oh?" Jason emptied his drink and waited. Bishop would make an excellent chess player; he was five steps ahead of Jason and already knew his next move.

"Francie said Sophie was chatting away about children and such when your sister entered, waving a letter you had sent her from America. When she said your name, Francie told me Ana gasped and went into a fit of choking, as though she could not breathe." Bishop's lips twitched. "While you might have stolen more than one woman's breath, I doubt you did it in this manner."

Could the man not just say what he was thinking and be done with it? "What are you implying?"

Bishop shrugged. "I have made a few assumptions based on my observations. I shall leave out the most obvious, such as the fabricated reason for her escape, and get to the more important ones. One, you and the woman who calls herself Ana Kendall have shared some sort of prior relationship. Two, William is nine, not eight, a fabrication she created only after she saw you. I would venture the boy's age contains a great secret that Ana has no desire to divulge." His silver gaze pierced Jason when he asked, "How am I doing?"

Blast, but the man was dead on. "You have achieved a certain degree of accuracy."

"Hmm. What degree, if I might inquire?"

"Were you a marksman, you would have hit a bull's-eye."

"As I suspected. I do have a third point, one you must be considering yourself. It is of a rather delicate nature and is only supposition, but it does beg one to ask the question and consider the ramifications."

"And that is?"

"Could you be William's father?"

***

"Will Mr. Trent visit today? Mr. Bishop taught me a new chess move and I want to try it out."

"Not today, William. Mr. Trent is busy with meetings and is not available. Perhaps he will pay you a visit tomorrow."

The boy smiled, his face lighting up in a way that reminded her too much of someone she wished to forget. William's hair was three shades lighter than Jason's, and thankfully, he had her eyes. Lady and Lord Nightingale both had chestnut hair and brown eyes, and the fairest of skin. The lack of resemblance to either "parent" confused William. Why did his hair not curl as Lord Nightingale's? And where were the freckles that splashed across Lady Nightingale's nose and cheeks? Ariana told him not all children were miniatures of their parents and that she had not resembled either her mother or father. Of course this was not true; she had looked like a younger version of her mother, but what was one more tale in a book of lies?

"Francie said a gentleman from America visited Mr. Trent last evening. She said his name is Jerome or Jeremy." He paused, scratched his chin, and mused, "Or Jason. I cannot remember, but he is a very good friend of Mr. Trent's. Did you meet him, too?"

Oh, yes, I have indeed met the man, and his name is Jason Langford. Your father. "I did meet him though we did not have a personal conversation." Why could the man not be an ocean away as she had thought? And why could he not have a big belly and a double chin with rude manners and a bald head? Why did he have to be more handsome than the Jason Langford she knew nine years ago? And what of the betrothed who by now should have been his wife? And children, where were they?

Ariana pulled William into her arms for a quick hug before releasing him. At nine, the boy did not like incessant hugging and his "mother" had done more than enough of that from the bed she was confined to for the last six months. How tragic that the woman had never quite been able to fully recover from the loss of so many babies, though she pretended well enough, and perhaps even had moments when she believed she had given birth to William.

"Did the man tell any stories of America?" William asked, his eyes bright with curiosity.

"I do not believe so." Jason Langford was more interested in trying to trap her with uncomfortable questions and pry into her past than share stories of his own.

"I should so enjoy speaking with him about it," William said. "Then I might compare what I have read to real life." His pale brows pulled into a straight line as he considered this. "I would wager a week of lemon cakes he has enjoyed high adventures at sea, mayhap a storm or two, and who knows what he has seen in America. You must ask Francie to invite him here."

Francie insisted the child call her by her given name and William had been more than pleased to comply. "It is not polite to ask someone to extend an invitation."

"But Francie would not mind. She likes company and I think she would enjoy the man's tales." He lowered his voice. "She has told me some that are very scary, but she said not to let Mr. Bishop know as he only wants her to think good thoughts until the baby comes. Francie said that was silly, that the baby loved hearing her scary stories." He tilted his head and looked up at her. "Do you think my mother told me scary stories when I was in her belly?"

No, your mother was too sad to tell you any stories. "I don't think Lady Nightingale liked scary stories." *And she is not your mother. I am. Me. Ariana Kendrick.*

"Do you think Father misses us?"

Ariana sucked in a breath to calm herself. From the moment she unpacked her small valise, Lord Nightingale had eyed her with equal parts contempt and desire. His frequent trips led him to Paris and Rome, even Vienna, leaving little time for him to grow acquainted with his "son" and even less to mend the tattered relationship with his wife. Ariana and Lady Nightingale became reluctant friends, two women who loved the same child and vowed to see him grow into a respectable young man. On her deathbed she warned Ariana that her husband could not be trusted with William's future—or with Ariana's honor. She advised her to remain vigilant and do what was necessary to protect her son. Three weeks after the woman's death, Ariana and William escaped.

"Well, do you think he misses us?" He paused, looked away. "Maybe misses me a little?"

How could a man miss a child he had spent nine years avoiding? Ariana smoothed her son's hair from his forehead and said, "I am sure he does, but for now, we need to stay here. Remember?"

"Uh-huh." He nodded but he did not look convinced.

"Tell me again why we had to leave." They had practiced this from the moment they left the estate until Alexander Bishop found them on the roadside four months ago.

"We had to leave because Father was grieving Mother so much he'd gone a bit mad."

"Yes, very good." Well, that is what they had recited but it was better than the truth. The horrible man had threatened to send William away to school unless Ariana became his mistress. *We're a family*, he'd said. *We belong together*. She had told him she needed time to consider the offer, and he had responded by dragging his gaze from her lips to her belly, settling on her breasts. *I have business in town and will return in three days. Share my bed or say good-bye to your son.* She and William left the next day.

"Do you think America has wild horses? I once read about them roaming the land. And wolves, and I believe lions as well."

"I do not believe America is a home for lions." She wished he would think of something other than America, but once William got an idea in his head, he would not release it until he had dissected every detail of it. She sighed. If only Jason Langford had remained in America, William might turn his inquisitiveness to Greece or Italy. Any location was preferable to a country that reminded her of her ex-lover.

Chapter 3

Jason waited most of the morning for a chance to confront Ariana, but he would wait a fortnight if it meant learning the details of her disappearance and why her family hung a black wreath on their door and told him she was dead. What had happened to change the plans they'd made to marry and raise a family in the country, where class rank made no difference? She'd only needed to wait until Christmas and then he would have announced his intention to marry her, first to his father and then her parents. There was to be no "asking," especially where the earl was concerned, for Edward Langford loved to control people, especially his children. This time was to have been different; this time Jason would stand up and fight for the one thing he believed in above all else: his love for Ariana.

But there had been no need for an announcement at all. His one true love was dead, according to her father, and there was nothing left to be said—except, apparently, there had been much left *unsaid*. What had forced Ariana's family to hang a black wreath on their door? A pregnancy, perhaps? Had Ariana carried his child and was that child William? Had the vicar tossed her out when she confessed she was with child? Not a particularly Christian act, but there were many hypocrites in this world. Had Jason been deprived of his right to know he had a son? There were too many questions swirling in his brain, creating an uncommon agitation. There was but one way to calm such agitation: obtain answers from Ariana. She would attempt to lie when faced with this last question, but Jason was adept at recognizing liars.

Alexander Bishop had been surprisingly helpful last night. Perhaps it was the drink or the urgency in Jason's voice that made the man suggest a plan to speak with Ariana at his residence, a plan that devoured Jason's sleep and made him past anxious for morning.

When Ariana arrived for her morning stroll in the gardens at the precise time Bishop quoted, Jason waited until she was deep in the maze of trimmed privet, far enough from the estate so as not to be heard or disturbed, and then he followed her. "Hello, Ariana." She swung around, her face pale, eyes wide. He moved toward her, closing the distance of nine years, and said, "You are looking exceedingly well—" he paused, forced a tight smile "—for a dead woman, that is."

"Why are you here?" She took a step back, then another, as if she could run from the truth.

Jason moved closer, did not stop until he was but an arm's length away. "I think you know."

"I do not, and it is improper for you to be here, unannounced and without benefit of a chaperone."

That made him laugh. "You were not always so insistent on a chaperone."

Her face changed from pale to a brilliant red. "A misstep of my youth, I can assure you." Those full lips flattened, spat out, "No proper gentleman would make such a comment, and I will thank you to cease such remarks at once."

He had always been attracted to her feisty nature and independent attitude. If he were not plagued with nine years of questions stuffed with lies and a boy who might be his, he might encourage further discourse that would elicit a similar response. "What is a proper gentleman, do tell? Have you much experience with them, or is Sebastian Trent the first?"

Those blue eyes looked as though they might shoot

flames at him. "Leave Mr. Trent out of this conversation."

"Ah, but I think he is a very important part of it." Jason crossed his arms over his chest and tried to ignore the faint lavender scent drifting toward him. He had once gifted Ariana with a box of lavender sachets and soaps, for which she'd thanked him with a kiss—long, slow, and filled with so many promises. "Sebastian is one person we have in common, is he not?" Before she could respond, he went on, "He has been my friend since childhood. You have known him less than four months."

"*He* is none of your business."

"I will not have you lying to him. Sebastian is a good man, but far too trusting. Does he have any idea who you really are? Or that you and I knew each other years ago?" He paused, added, "Intimately?"

"Of course not! I do not care to relive the past or my mistakes."

"How very convenient for you." Could she really manipulate the past in such a manner as to "forget" it, or even "re-work" it to achieve a different outcome?

The bland expression on her face indicated she could and intended to do just that. Ariana lifted her chin and eyed him with an air that might have marked *her* the one with noble blood, and him, the peasant. "If you will excuse me, I must get back to Drakemoor."

"I see. Running away again." A surge of anger shot through him. She might have run from him nine years ago and let him believe she was dead, but by God, he would have answers before she ran this time.

"I could say the same of you—" she paused, stared at him "—if I were interested in your lies and subterfuge, but what would be the point? The past is gone and I have paid dearly for holding onto childish dreams."

"*My* lies and subterfuge? You let me think you were dead."

"And you were betrothed."

"What? I was never betrothed." What the hell was she talking about? "The woman I planned to marry was dead...or I thought she was."

"Please do not say that." She took a step backward, then another as if to pull away from the words he had just uttered.

"Why not? Does the truth make you uncomfortable or would you prefer to forget that we planned to marry?"

She shook her head and waves of red curls danced about her shoulders, settled along her breasts. He had touched that hair, buried his face in those curls. "You never intended to marry me. It was all a lie." Her voice cracked, split open with what sounded an awful lot like pain. "You let me think you wanted to marry me...but you did not."

"Ariana." He placed his hands on her shoulders, said in a gentle voice, "I *did* want to marry you."

Her eyes grew bright, brighter still. "Your father," she whispered.

"My father? What about him?"

A tear slipped down her cheek, then another, but she did not try to stop them. "He sent for me, told me I must leave the village at once and if I refused, he would destroy my family." She blinked hard, looked away. "He said you had no interest in me other than seduction, and then he told me you were betrothed."

"Damn him!"

"Why would I not believe he would do as he said when he'd sent his oldest son away because the boy embarrassed him? The entire village feared your father, and none of us trusted him to show a kindness when he could not show one to his own family."

"He must have found out about us. But how?"

She shrugged, looked away. "Perhaps someone saw us."

His father was a cruel man, but forcing a woman from her family for loving his son was beyond harsh. Unless there was a more compelling reason to send her away. "Ariana, look at me."

She dragged her gaze to meet his. "Yes?"

He could well and truly lose himself in the blueness of those eyes, but she was a liar and he would do well to remember that. "Is William my son?"

"No!" She stepped out of reach, her expression one of shock. "William is not your son."

There had been a time when he knew what she was thinking before she spoke, and her words were pure and honest. But now? He studied her face, heard her denial, and could not say if she spoke the truth. Still, if he wasn't the father, who was? "If not me, then who?"

Ariana looked away. "Jason. Please."

"If your son is indeed nine years old, either he is mine or you hopped out of my bed and into someone else's." The thought that she could forget him so easily made his chest ache. "Well, which is it?"

"You are not the father," she said, her voice thin, yet determined. "When your father cast me from my village, I found work far away from Ellswood as a governess. The earl had a sickly wife, and he…and we…"

"Good God." He had never thought her capable of sleeping with another woman's husband, and the knowledge that she had made the truth so much worse.

"I paid dearly for my indiscretions. Apparently, the earl's wife was barren, yet longed for a child, even one that was not from her womb. She and the earl had concocted a scheme in which he would impregnate a woman they both chose, then threaten to take the child once it was born and never let the woman see it again. However, the woman would be permitted to remain with the family as the child's governess and the earl's wife would be its mother."

"That is the sickest tale I have ever heard."

"What choice does a woman like me have against a wealthy nobleman and his wife?" Her nostrils flared, her lips flattened seconds before she continued, "It was not much different than the bargain your father forced on me. Wealth trumps the poor, every single time."

The stories she had told him were tangled with deceit and betrayal. What was true and what was not, and how would he ever be able to tell the difference? "What happened to the earl and his wife?"

"She died." Ariana clutched her cloak about her and said, "And he determined we should continue as a 'family,' with me in his bed instead of down the hall."

Her words sounded sincere, but were they, or did they only appear so because he wanted to believe them? "Is that when you left?"

She nodded. "Yes."

"And William will substantiate this?"

Anger spilled from her next words. "I am not on trial and you will not use my son to determine the truth of my story."

"I would like to meet William." There was something about this tale that did not fit, like a wrong-sized boot.

"I think not."

"Why?" Jason forced a smile and pointed to his head. "Does he have hair the color of a wheat field? Or a nose like this?" He held out his hands, flexed them. "Or mayhap, does his thumb bend to the right a bit like this?"

Ariana moved away from him, slowly, precisely, one

step at a time. "I shall thank you to leave my son out of your imaginings. He does not look like you, Jason. Not. One. Bit."

Her words spilled out in an anxious rush that did little to make him believe her. "Under the circumstances, I am sure you can understand why I might want to take a look for myself. Of course, I will not tell him why I have an interest in his hair or the way he walks." He paused, took a step toward her. "We'll keep that our little secret for now. No sense upsetting anyone about a past relationship we would just as soon forget, right?" *I will never be able to forget you, even though you broke my heart.*

"Yes, absolutely. I certainly have no intention of telling anyone."

"Because it did not mean anything, right?"

She met his gaze, held it so long he almost looked away. "Exactly."

That was not an answer. There was no point pressing her any further about anything because Ariana Kendrick was not admitting anything. He would have to unearth the truth himself and he would accept the help of a most unlikely but capable ally—Alexander Bishop. The man had tremendous analytical capabilities and if they worked together, Jason was certain they could learn the secrets Ariana kept hidden—his father's part in this whole mess, her plans for Sebastian, and why she did not want him to meet William, the boy she claimed was not his.

***

"Do you not think Jason Langford is handsome?" Francie and Ariana sat at a table in the drawing room with bunches of lavender spread out before them. Francie had been teaching Ariana to weave the lavender in a grapevine wreath to make a fetching and fragrant decoration. The woman grew her own garden of flowers and tended it, too. Quite a rarity, considering she had servants aplenty for the task. That, and the fact that she was heavy with child. "Well?"

Oh, why did that man's name have to pop up, just when Ariana had begun to relax and had not thought of Jason Langford for all of ten seconds? The man was a veritable pest who would not go away. Did she think him handsome? He was more than handsome with his gray eyes, slow smiles, and wheat-colored hair that swept about his neck. And then there were his shoulders, broad chest, narrow hips, and long legs. Attractive indeed. But Ariana would choke before she uttered such words. "I had not noticed."

Francie paused, a sprig of lavender in one hand, and turned to Ariana. "You had not noticed? Truly?" And then, "How could you *not* have noticed? The man is exquisite, with an agreeable personality to boot."

Ariana shrugged. "Perhaps." She would *not* notice anything remotely appealing about the man. She simply would not.

Laughter spilled from Francie. "You must be the only woman in the countryside who has not noticed Jason Langford's attributes. I daresay, there will be many invitations for tea and such once news of his return has spread through the area."

Ariana grabbed two sprigs of lavender. "Then he shall have his fill of tea and conversation."

More laughter. "Indeed he shall." Francie snatched a cookie from the plate the Bishops' butler had delivered earlier. She chewed and nodded as if considering Ariana's comments, and then said, "Sebastian will make a wonderful father."

Where had that come from? "Sebastian? Why are you

talking about him? Were you not just discussing the merits of Jason Langford?"

"Yes, but now I am interested in Sebastian and what kind of father he will be to William." She snatched another cookie. "Quite excellent, I believe. He is a man of great patience, kindness, and empathy, all necessary traits in a good father."

Patience, kindness, empathy? Did Francie believe Alexander Bishop, the father of her children, possessed such qualities? Ariana had not known the man overlong, but she would not have used those words to describe him. Apparently, a woman in love had a much different perspective than a casual acquaintance.

"Have you chosen a date for the wedding?"

Ariana's stomach jumped and churned at the question. "No, we have not, but we will. Soon." She blocked visions of Jason Langford from her brain. He had no business intruding on her thoughts, or her sleep, as he had done last evening. It was Sebastian she should be thinking of…Sebastian whose arms should be holding her…Sebastian whose lips should be covering hers…

"The date will not come soon enough for Sebastian." Francie slid her a smile. "I see the way he watches you, as though you are a goddess and he is your servant. It is lovely to witness, and I am so pleased you have found each other." She patted Ariana's hand and nodded with confidence. "You are good for him, Ana."

My name is not Ana. It is Ariana. And I am not certain you would think I was good for him if you knew the truth about me. "Thank you."

"Too many women tried to win favor with him in hopes of securing a proposal, but they did not really care about him. Oh, they might have paid him pretty compliments, and a few even visited his mother in hopes she would persuade her son to look their way, but in the end, Sebastian saw through their scheming ways." Francie lifted another cookie from the plate, nibbled on it. "But you are not like them, Ana. You are true and honest, and you will make Sebastian a most excellent wife."

***

"Have you solved the mystery yet?"

Jason scowled at Alexander Bishop, who did not appear the least intimidated by the look, and said, "No, I have not, and that blasted woman is making it bloody difficult to secure answers."

"Then you must find another avenue to obtain your information."

Bishop had invited him for a morning ride, one that began before the sun had an opportunity to warm the air or the field under his horse's hooves. But Jason had not refused the offer; he'd been feeling a bit "closed in" since his arrival from America, and had need of a large stretch of land where his horse could run flat out, and the brisk air could fill Jason's lungs, and Alexander Bishop might offer a bit of advice to hasten answers from Ariana. Bishop had a keen eye and he had been watchful.

"Would you be so kind as to suggest another avenue, for I have run into a wall." Jason eased his horse alongside Bishop's and waited for the man to offer his next strategy. Alexander Bishop might appear a stuffed shirt, but he had a heart, though he preferred not to reveal it to anyone but his wife. He also possessed the ability to analyze situations in great detail, considering areas others might have missed. This served him well in the stock market and in the business of people and their motives.

Right now, Jason needed his help with Ariana and *her*

motives, be they true or fabricated for her own benefit.

"Is it not obvious?" Bishop slid him a sidelong glance. "You must secure a meeting with William and ask him questions, but not such pointed ones that he will become suspicious and clamp down on information like a pointer with a duck in its mouth. Inquire about the boy's hobbies, his favorite dessert; ask if he likes animals. When you have drawn him into your confidence and he is chattering away, as he is prone to do, ask him his father's name. If done properly, the boy will not even know he has offered up valuable and secure information."

"Interesting ploy." It was Jason's turn to study Bishop. "Used it yourself a time or two, haven't you?"

The man actually smiled. Not a twitch of lips or a fleeting half smile, but a full-blown one. Most interesting. "I have had need to use the tactic on occasion."

"And did you achieve success?"

The smile spread. "Absolutely."

Jason waited to hear more, but when they rode several moments in silence, it became obvious there would be no elaboration. "Ariana insists I am not William's father."

"And you believe her?"

Jason shrugged. What he did and did not believe was as murky as the pond where he and Holt used to look for fish when they were children. "She refuses to let me see the boy. How can I look for similarities if I cannot even see the chap?"

"Patience is key, and you must remain calm."

"I would like to see how calm you would be if it were your son we were talking about."

Bishop pierced him with that damnable silver gaze. "I do not think you would want to see. As a matter of fact, I guarantee you would not."

"To hell with what I would and would not want to see; are you going to help me?" If William were his, he would be damned if another man, even a good one like Sebastian Trent, would raise the boy as his own.

Bishop slowed his horse and turned to Jason. "You will have an opportunity to meet the boy. When you do, I suggest you study the lobes of his ears. Small. Thin." He glanced at Jason's ears. "Look also at his teeth. And the set of his jaw. Offer him something to eat and observe the manner in which he chews from one side of his mouth to the other. If you follow these instructions, you will know if William is your son."

"The manner in which he chews?" Jason repeated. "What the devil will that prove?" Was the man daft? In what possible manner could chewing and the set of a jaw prove one's parentage? Bishop merely shrugged and repeated the instructions as though Jason were the one who was daft for not understanding them.

"Come to Drakemoor tomorrow at two o'clock. William will be waiting, and then you shall have your answer."

Tomorrow was too many hours away and Jason had questions now, buckets of them. "And if the boy is mine, how will I get her to admit it?"

Bishop smiled again, the second time this morning. "That is where strategy comes in." He paused, and damn but the man winked. "My specialty."

57

Chapter 4

Jason opened the library door and slipped inside. Alexander Bishop had been waiting for him when the butler ushered Jason into Drakemoor. What an odd creature the butler was, with his foot tapping and nose twitching. Perhaps the man had been around Francie Bishop's animals too long and had taken up imitating them. This particular habit resembled a rabbit and according to Julia, there was indeed a rabbit hopping about the interior of the mansion.

How did Alexander Bishop tolerate such nonsense? He must truly love his wife for he did not appear the type to permit clutter, confusion, or chaos in his life or his household. Francie Bishop, on the other hand, seemed to not only enjoy but thrive in the aforementioned environments.

Bishop had instructed him to arrive in mid-afternoon, a quiet time when the other children were napping and Ariana and Francie were preoccupied with gardening projects. Jason did not see the boy until he was well into the room. William sat propped on a stack of pillows, shaggy head bent, fists under his chin, a book resting on his knees. He did not look up until Jason spoke.

"Hello. Are you William?"

The boy's head shot up, a mix of surprise and curiosity on his face. "I am. What's your name?"

"Jason Langford." He hesitated, added, "I am a friend of Mr. Bishop's." Perhaps "friend" was a bit of a stretch, but it would have to suffice.

William's blue eyes sparkled. They were two shades lighter than Ariana's. "You're Julia's brother!" His voice dipped, swirled with excitement, when he said, "And that makes you the Earl of Westover's brother, the one everybody says was a pirate." The voice dipped further. "Is it true? Was your brother a pirate?"

Jason shrugged. "My brother never said and I doubt he will." There was much mystery surrounding his brother's past and Holt had yet to reveal it, which could mean the past would remain shrouded with questions and unknowns for the foreseeable future, perhaps forever. Jason knew about keeping the past in its place and had no interest in resurrecting his brother's or his own. Unless the past came calling in the form of an ex-lover and a boy who could be his child...then the situation required investigation and action.

"Are you the brother who lived in America?"

Inquisitive little bugger. "I am. Did my sister tell you that tale?"

The boy nodded, his smile spreading across his face, stretching almost to his ears, ears with *small lobes*. "She wants to go there and ride horses bareback, wear breeches instead of gowns, and leather." His head bobbed in thought. "Lots of leather."

"Of course she does." Julia was still Julia, outrageous and outspoken, with far too many opinions. "You should not listen to my sister for she is a master storyteller of fairy tales."

"I like her, but Mr. Bishop says odds are she will remain a spinster; Francie disagrees. She says there is a special someone for Julia, just as there is for everyone. All they need do is keep their eyes open, remain patient, and let the magic work."

That sounded like a concoction of rubbish that might spill from Francie Bishop's lips. Magic indeed. What would she say if she knew about Jason and Ariana's past? Would she wish magic on them as well? He sank into the chair beside the mountain of pillows William perched upon and said, "Do you like living here?"

The boy nodded. "Very much." He paused, added, "I especially like Francie's animals. Have you ever met Miss Penelope? She's a rabbit and can eat right out of my hand."

"I do not believe I've had occasion to meet her." And if he were lucky, he would never have occasion to do so.

William scurried to his feet, stood next to Jason's chair, and blurted out, "Would you like to meet her? She's very soft and likes to hide under the furniture. I believe she's in the drawing room with Francie and Ari—I mean, Mother. I could show you, if you like."

"I do not wish to disturb your mother at present. She might be busy and it is not polite to intrude uninvited."

"Oh." His mouth pulled into a frown. "I guess that means we cannot see George either, or Mr. Pib since they are usually at Francie's feet."

The dog and the cat. "Perhaps next time." He eyed the boy, noted the strong nose, the pale blond hair. Jason might be able to claim parts of William's ear, and maybe the teeth, but what else? His gut told him William was his son, but could he prove it? He must learn more about the boy's circumstance. "Do you miss your father?"

The child's eyes grew wide with something that could only be described as fear. "My father?"

"Yes. Mr. Bishop said he's gone." Jason waited until the boy's shoulders relaxed and added a most convincing lie. "Dead. Problem with the heart."

"Yes." The word spilled out, but its uncertainty hung between them.

"What is it, William? Is something wrong?" *Tell me, tell me all about it.*

"I—" he looked away, dropped his gaze on his shoes "—'tis nothing."

Oh, but it was something and that something held a significance to all involved, including the supposed dead father. "William." He worked his voice into a sympathetic tone. "It's obvious you're not being honest with me." The sudden spurt of red on the boy's face confirmed the deduction. "I am sure you have a very good reason; maybe you're protecting someone—" he paused and waited for William to meet his gaze before he continued. "You are an honorable person, I can tell. But whatever secret you are keeping is weighing on your young shoulders. If you trust me with that secret, I might be able to help you."

William swallowed hard, his thin shoulders sagging with guilt and uncertainty. "I promised to keep the secret."

Jason rubbed his chin, waited. "Even if it is not the truth?" he ventured. "Even if it puts others in danger or is unfair to them?" *Even if the truth keeps a father from his son?*

Those eyes grew wide and bright. "I don't want to put anyone in danger. Do you think I did?"

"How can I say when I do not know the secret?" *He was so close...*

William's small face creased with worry. "Perhaps you should talk to...my mother."

A conversation with Ariana about William's father would prove as unfruitful as the last one, of that he was certain. "Do you not wish to protect your mother?"

"Of course I do."

"Then, the logical action would be to disclose information that would ensure her protection, would it not?"

"Yes?"

Was that a "yes" or a "no" that sounded like a yes? "Very well then." He studied the boy's face, searching for further indications he was a Langford. The shape of the eyebrows was similar. And the small dimple on the right side of his face when he smiled. Perhaps the cowlick that brushed over his forehead. Nothing significant, but when pieced together, they could make a strong case. And the set of William's jaw was indeed that of a Langford.

"My father is not dead," he blurted out.

Finally. "He's not?"

William shook his head and spat out more secrets. "My mother is dead. Ari—Ana is my governess." His eyes filled with tears. "Her real name is Ariana. She has always taken care of me, from the time I was a baby. My mother was sickly and spent much time in bed." He sniffed, swiped his hands over his face. "We never saw Father unless his friends visited from the city, but that was not very often. A few weeks after Mother's funeral, I heard him and Ariana fighting. I know I should not have listened, but I was scared." Tears slipped from his cheeks to his chin, then along his neck, but he did not try to stop them. "Father threatened to send me away if Ariana did not do what he wanted, but I could not hear what that was. He said he would separate us and she would never see me again. Why would he say that?"

Jason pulled the boy into his arms. *Damn the man who made this child fear for his home and safety.* "People can be cruel." Had his father not disregarded him and Julia and sent Holt away to a crazy uncle? "The cruelty is their lacking, not yours." He eased away and reached into his jacket pocket, pulled out a chocolate. "Here, this will make you feel better."

"Thank you." William unwrapped the chocolate, popped it in his mouth, and chewed, first on one side of his mouth and then the other. Jason recalled Alexander's words. *Look also at his teeth. And the set of his jaw. Offer him something to eat and observe the manner in which he chews from one side of his mouth to the other. If you follow these instructions, you will know if William is your son.*

Jason handed his son another chocolate and watched him chew. Had the act of chewing ever made him so happy? He did not think so. "No one will hurt you, William. Rest assured, your family will protect you. Of that you may be certain."

A short while later, Jason left the library with a promise to visit William again soon, at which time he would share his adventures in America. He had years to make up for and did not wish to lose another moment. Oh, but Ariana had much explaining to do, beginning with the truth about the mysterious earl who had threatened to send William away. There was much more to this story, and Jason would hear all of it before night's end.

He threw open the drawing room door and stalked toward the woman he had thought long dead. She had deceived him, broken his heart, and cheated him of his son. "Out," Jason said to the butler who stood next to the table where Ariana sat, his arms laden with what looked like wreaths made of sticks. The man mumbled something, dropped the wreaths, and scurried away.

Ariana stared at Jason, lips flattened, eyes narrowed, fingers clutching bunches of lavender. "I spoke with William." He ignored the speed with which her face paled and lifted a sprig of lavender, twirled it between his fingers and brought it to his nose. "Such a deceptive scent, like the wearer, don't you agree?" They had lain in a field of lavender the first time they made love; he had thought that love would last through a marriage, children, and a final resting place side by side in St. Andrew's cemetery. Oh, how wrong he had been.

"Stay away from my son."

"*Your* son?" He advanced on her, making his way around the table to stand less than an arm's length from her. "Interesting choice of words." He leaned close enough to see the almost invisible smattering of freckles along her nose. "I believe you mean *our* son."

Those eyes glared at him, attempting to burn holes in his words. "William is my son. I raised him."

"Because I had no knowledge of his existence, a situation I intend to rectify at once."

"But you cannot just—"

"Oh, but I can," he spat out, his anger permeating each word. "And I will."

***

What had happened to the Jason Langford who had scribbled lines of poetry, professed his love and devotion, and swore they would grow old together, hand in hand? That young man had disappeared and been replaced with one who did not appear to have a heart for past loves, forgiveness, or second chances. And he most certainly had no patience for anything bordering on a fabrication, even a necessary one.

"Speak, Ariana, and I am not interested in any more of your lies, no matter how good-intentioned you might think they are." He leaned against the edge of the table, crossed his arms over his broad chest, and stared at her. "I lost my patience with you the moment you walked into Sebastian's drawing room and I realized you were still alive but chose to let me believe you were dead. You have woven so many lies I have no idea what is true and what is not." His voice dipped, turned hard. "But know this, before I quit this room, I will know the truth, and I will have it verified by the sources I have secured for this very purpose."

"You think to cause me fear?" She glared back at him, wishing him to hell three times over. "Do all Langfords believe they can force their wishes upon others, or is it only the ones who are weak in heart and spirit who choose to bully the less fortunate? You want, therefore, I must obey? Rubbish to that. I shall give you the truth, all of it, and then I shall bid you good riddance."

His full lips stretched into a thin smile. "Not very likely."

"We shall see." She stood and made her way to the other end of the table, far enough away so he could not touch her but close enough to stand her ground. "Here is a bit of truth for you. The earl I spoke of who told me I could either give up my child to his friend or he would destroy my family? That was your father." She waited for his response, but he did not say a word and showed no emotion, as though he had not heard her. Not even a twitch of jaw or a flaring of nostril. "Did you hear what I said? The man who sent me away and threatened my family—"

"I heard you." And then, "You could find no way to attempt to contact me? I could have stopped this madness and kept you from leaving." The tiniest bit of pain slipped into his voice. "I could have helped you."

If he believed that, then he was a fool, a dreamer, or an innocent. "How would you have done that, Jason? Your father shipped your brother from his home like he was a piece of beef to be traded. What kind of man does that? What kind of man threatens to destroy a woman's family if she does not follow his wishes? You could no more have stopped your father from sending me away than Holt could remain at Ellswood."

Jason pushed away from the table and moved toward her. "He discovered you were carrying my child, didn't he?

That is why he sent you away and why he threatened you."

"Yes." There was no point pretending it were not so. Jason knew William was his son and while she might continue to refute his claim, her denial would grow weaker as his insistence strengthened.

"The story of your indiscretion with the earl and his wife's demand that the child call her Mother while you took the position as his governess, was that necessary?" He slashed a hand in the air. "You would wish such a situation on yourself, and for what purpose? So I would not learn I had a son?"

"While I might have lied about a liaison with the earl, I did not fabricate the rest of the horrid story. *That* was the bargain I struck with your father to protect my family."

His face twisted with equal parts anger and disgust. "Are you saying you actually played the part of governess while an earl and his wife pretended to be William's parents?"

"Does the idea disgust you?" She advanced on him, clenching her fists so she did not lash out at his face. "Imagine what I felt like to know the baby I carried would never call me Mother? I was not even permitted to name him." She let out a cold laugh and spat out, "Your father was quite thorough with his instructions and I learned a good deal of coin exchanged hands, and it fell straight into your father's pockets."

"I…" He rubbed a hand over his face, sighed. "I would like to tell you I do not believe it, but too many years with my father indicate this is indeed exactly what he would do." There was true concern on his face when he asked, "Did you ever find even a modicum of happiness or contentment these past years?"

"In a way, I did." She shrugged. "But how can one be truly happy when one's own child calls another Mother?"

Ariana let this one small truth slip out. "It was more painful than I care to remember."

"And the part you told me about the earl vowing to send William away if you did not agree to share his bed? Was that true?"

She did not miss the twitch on the left side of his jaw when he spoke. "Unfortunately, yes."

"I am truly sorry for your misfortunes and my father's part in it. You have but to give me the earl's name and I will see he never bothers you again."

"What would you do? Challenge him to a duel?"

Those gray eyes pierced her. "If necessary."

Was he mad? This business of dueling to defend a woman's honor was no more than a bucket of rubbish and she wanted no part of it. "I cannot imagine a woman encouraging her defender to risk his life for the sake of supposed honor. It is ridiculous."

"You would care if I suffered an injury?"

She did not miss the humor in his voice, but there was a hint of something else, too—curiosity? Hope? "I would not want Francie's Mr. Pib to suffer an injury, and he's a cat."

"Of course I should have known you would place me in the same category as an animal."

"Consider yourself fortunate." Her lips twitched. "Mr. Pib is held in high regard at Drakemoor."

"No doubt, especially with Francie Bishop as its mistress." His lips pulled into a smile and he confessed, "Duels are not my style. I have always preferred to use my wits to a weapon."

"Indeed?"

"It has been said my wits are sharper than a sword and more deadly than a pistol."

She laughed, a real laugh, not a concoction put to sound

for the benefit of the listener. When he spoke thus, he reminded her of the Jason Langford of long ago, the one who teased and intrigued…tempted and pleasured…*Goodness, where had that last thought come from and how could she quash any more from popping into her brain?*

"I would like to see William again. Perhaps I could take him riding tomorrow?" he asked, his smile making her stomach flip-flop. "After his lessons, of course." Pause. "Would you like to accompany us?"

"No. But thank you." She could not accompany Jason Langford on a horse ride with their son. Absolutely not. While it may appear as though the man were merely offering a bit of attention to a young boy who had recently lost his father, that was not the case. *He* was William's father and that placed them in an awkward situation, one that threatened to bring back unwanted memories should they find themselves in each other's company for too long. Why, in the short expanse of time she had found herself in his presence, had she not suffered a jumpy stomach, an ache in her chest, a pinch in her temple, and a problem gathering a full breath? That did not constitute a healthy situation for her brain or her body…certainly not her heart.

She was betrothed to Sebastian Trent, a good and kind man, who would not hurt her or make her weep in misery. One must love another with a desperateness to create such pain, and she had learned her lesson well. *Do not risk the heart, do not risk the pain.*

"When will you tell Sebastian the truth?"

Ariana dragged her gaze to the man who had broken her heart and forced out the words. "In time."

"You cannot marry him."

"Cannot?" *He will not break my heart.*

His expression turned fierce. "What does the man really know about you, other than the obvious?" He raked a gaze from her face to her slippers and settled on her lips. "Does he know you are a vicar's daughter, or that you lived nearby? And what of the arrangement you had with the earl and his wife? What lies did you mix with that tale?"

"Sebastian knows what is important."

He advanced on her, stopped when his boots hit the hem of her gown. "And what exactly is that?"

She attempted to back up, but the edge of the table dug into her back. "That I will make him a good wife," she replied, lifting her chin. "That I will do my best to make him happy."

"Hmm. Such honorable endeavors, but they shall be difficult to achieve when mired in secrets. Sebastian needs to know the truth—" he paused, his nostrils flaring "—all of it."

She knew what he meant and while she wanted to ignore his words, he was right. Sebastian deserved to learn the truth about Ariana and Jason and the son they shared. "I thought I had suffered enough and had finally found a home and peace. How could I possibly know Sebastian was your friend? Moreover, word had it you lived in America these past two years and had no intention of returning. I thought myself safe." She shook her head, stared at his mouth. "But I shall never be safe from you."

"I never meant to hurt you," he said, his voice rough, almost tortured.

"But you did." When she met his gaze, she tried to ignore the pain in his eyes. Perhaps she had not been the only one who had suffered from his father's cruelty.

"Ariana," he whispered, seconds before he pulled her into his arms, his mouth covering hers, coaxing her lips open. When she moaned, his tongue dipped inside. She could not think, could not consider anything but the taste of his tongue on hers, the feel of his strong body pressed against her, close, closer. He eased her onto the table, amidst the lavender and ribbons, one hand buried in her hair, another trailing from her cheek, to her neck, to her breasts. Another moan escaped her, this one louder, needier, as she flung her hands behind his neck and pulled him to her. Oh, but it had been such a long time, and while Sebastian might prove a skilled lover, he was too much the gentleman to press for more than a chaste kiss on the cheek.

But the truth was that no matter his skill or his competence, he was not Jason Langford. Nobody was. She sighed, closed her eyes, and arched her back to allow him greater access to the front of her bodice. Jason's hand stilled, followed by a curse and then the weight of his body pressing into hers was gone. Ariana opened her eyes, ignoring the bits of lavender clinging to her hair and gown, and moved into a sitting position. "Jason?" He looked past angry; he looked furious, and it was directed at her.

He stood several feet away, jaw set, fists clenching and unclenching. "You would consider marrying another man, yet you allow me to kiss you, touch you—" he gestured to the table where she sat "—allow me to spread you out like a dessert? Either you have turned into a loose woman and succumb to the touch of any man, or you still have feelings for me. I would know the answer to that, but first, you will break it off with Sebastian, for either way you will not marry my friend."

Chapter 5

Ariana's father had preached to his parish about the importance of behaving honorably and with grace, thinking of others instead of oneself, and never losing hope, not even in the bleakest of hours. He brought these sentiments into their home, sat near the fire on cold nights with his family huddled close, and told stories of ordinary men and women whose faith transcended them to a higher level where all things were possible.

Oh, but Father would be disappointed in her now. She had lied to Sebastian, taken advantage of his kindness and good nature for purely selfish reasons. Ariana wanted security and protection for William, and while the reasons might be commendable, the methods were not. Had Jason not returned home and confronted her with her duplicity, she might have married Sebastian with the thought of telling him the truth at a later date. But there would be no later date; she knew that as well as she knew William's middle name was Matthew.

And what of poor William? How long would she let him believe his real mother was a noblewoman who had died? And what would she tell him about his father? Or rather, what would she tell his father about *him*? Everything? Nothing? Lies built upon lies, sinking into a quagmire, buried but never forgotten. There had been a time when the biggest untruth weighing on her conscience had been whether she had said her daily prayers. Then she met Jason Langford, and the lies churned into deeper ones as she stole away to meet him, doing things no maiden should do, and yet unable to stop herself.

It was because of him she had lost her home, her family, her hope for a life of happiness. She lost the ability to have her son call her Mother and that had been the greatest loss of all. But she could spare Sebastian before she pulled him so far into her lies he would suffocate. A man whose greatest fault was trusting others too much did not deserve that.

When she arrived at Sebastian's, the butler ushered her into the library, her betrothed's favorite room, one he considered calming and restorative. They had shared many a discussion here and it was in this very room that he helped William hone his chess skills. She should coax Sebastian to a different location, perhaps even a stroll out of doors so he need not look back at the spot where she revealed such hurtful truths, and see only betrayal.

"Sebastian?" Ariana forced a smile and moved toward his desk. "I am sorry to intrude, but I must speak with you."

He rose from the desk, his handsome face a mix of worry and compassion. For her. She did not deserve his worry or his compassion, and once he learned the truth, she would lose both. "Ana? What is it? You look unwell."

Oh, Sebastian, I am about to break your heart. She cleared her throat and pushed out the words that would begin the destruction of the fragile relationship they shared. "There are things I have not told you; truths you must know and should have known before you proposed."

He held her hands between his own and said in the gentlest of voices, "Do not dwell on the past. It will serve no purpose. Whatever manner of horrors you were subjected to are over, and I will not let that man hurt you again." His words turned fierce, determined. "You have but to say the word and I will deliver that message to him myself."

She shook her head. "No. I would not have you involved." *And that is but a small piece in this giant puzzle of lies.* "Besides, he is not the person I wish to discuss."

Ariana glanced about the room Sebastian so loved and said, "Might we take a stroll along the grounds? The trees are turning delightful shades and I would like to walk with you." If she delivered the news out of doors, at least Sebastian's home would not be marked with the memories of what she was about to say.

"Of course." He released her hands, stroked her cheek. "Anything for you." He paused, his eyes bright, and murmured, "My love."

Mercy, but she could not let him utter such words only to spear him with those very same ones once he learned the truth. "There is much I need to tell you. Please say no more until you have heard it all." *Pray when I am finished you will find it in your heart to forgive me.*

Sebastian nodded and helped her into her cloak. He remained silent until they had reached the south border of the estate, an area covered with bushes and trees whose leaves had turned to red, orange, and gold. Roses climbed white trellises, their red and pink blooms faded or absent, leaving the glossiness of their leaves to provide one final attraction.

"Well?" Sebastian stopped next to a trellis and faced Ariana. "We are out of doors as you wished; now please tell me what worries you."

"I cannot marry you," she blurted out.

His expression remained blank save for the twitch on the left side of his jaw. "I see."

"No, I do not believe you do." She willed him to understand. "I have not told you the truth about my situation. In fact, I have lied about most of it and for that, I am deeply sorry. My name is Ariana Kendrick; my father was the vicar in the village. I—" she swallowed, fought the embarrassment of the situation and pushed on "—met a young man and we…he…"

"Got you with child?"

"Yes."

"And you pretended to be a widow?" he ventured.

She nodded. "I waited for him to return from Oxford so I could tell him about the baby. He said he loved me and we would marry, but…"

"This young man, he was of noble birth?"

"The second son of an earl."

"I see."

"I know what you are thinking. The second son of an earl is not interested in marrying the daughter of a vicar, and if he has spent time with her, it was not to secure a proposal, at least not one of marriage."

Sebastian frowned. "Why do you speak so poorly of yourself? If you say the man intended to marry you, then I have no doubt that was his intention. However, something or someone intervened to prevent that."

"His father."

"Ah, there is always a father out to protect his offspring, or rather, the family name."

"He threatened to destroy my family, said he would ruin all of us." The story poured out then, all of it, except the name of the offending family, and ended with Ariana swiping at her face. She had stopped crying over her situation years ago, but telling someone who had no idea of her circumstances made it all return, as painful as when it first happened.

"Your own son was not permitted to call you Mother?"

She sniffed. "No."

"And you had no contact with your family all these years?"

She shook her head. "The family who employed me

forbade it, as did the earl who made the deal." Ariana paused and spat out, "He told me he would be paid handsomely for procuring a child. What kind of uncaring person would do such a thing?"

"A monster. Sadly, that type of manipulation happens far too often in our society and I am embarrassed to admit it."

Jason's father had indeed been a monster, but he was dead and could not threaten her or William. Lord Nightingale, however, was still lurking somewhere. "I fear the man I ran from will find me and try to claim William as his son." She blinked hard and said, "William believes they were his parents and he believes I am merely his governess."

"Then you best tell him the truth, and soon."

"What a horrible predicament I have gotten myself into, but that is my problem, not yours. I am very sorry for lying to you. Can you ever forgive me?"

Sebastian grasped her hands and said in a voice filled with compassion, "It is not for me to forgive that which I might have done myself were I in a similar predicament. You did what you had to in order to protect your family and your child." He squeezed her hands, his lips pulling into a smile. "You are a woman of great courage, Ariana Kendrick, and my feelings for you have not changed. Neither has my offer."

If Jason Langford had not arrived and accused her of taking advantage of his friend's trusting nature, she might well have gone through with the wedding. But drat it all, the man had been right; whether knowingly or not, she had taken advantage of Sebastian's kind-hearted, trusting nature and convinced herself she could make up for it by becoming an exemplary wife. That was the biggest lie of all.

"Have you nothing to say?"

Of course she had much to say, beginning with her true feelings toward him, which did not include love. "You are the most honorable man I know and I am quite fond of you, never doubt that."

His smile slipped a bit. "Ah, fondness, the death knell of a relationship."

"Oh, Sebastian, I am so very sorry."

He reached out, touched her cheek. "I pursued you; there is no need to apologize." The smile returned, accompanied by a sadness around his eyes. "My wounds will heal with the other scars I carry."

"I wish my answer could be different." She did wish this, with her whole heart.

"Might I hope that, in time, your feelings could change?"

Too many women pretended to have feelings for their betrotheds and husbands where none existed. She would not be one of them. "You deserve more than I can give, and I am only sorry it has taken me this long to realize it."

"Do not be sorry for admitting the truth." He paused. "And what of William's father? Is there hope for the two of you?"

Ariana met his gaze, held it. "How can there be hope when there is so much hurt and so many years of lies between us?"

"True love finds a way."

How difficult it must be for Sebastian to utter such words. "True love, yes, but false love, or the mistaken belief of love? That drowns with the first tide of misfortune."

***

When Jason paid a visit to Sebastian the next afternoon, he knew something was amiss the moment he saw him. Only once in all the years they had been friends had Sebastian lost his temper, and not merely to cursing and yelling, but he'd pounded his fist into a wall with such force and repetition, he'd bloodied and bruised his knuckles and could not use his hand to full capacity for six days. It was not until weeks later, when the damage from the incident had healed, that Sebastian divulged the reason for such behavior. His steadfast companion, an English pointer, had caught his back leg in a trap and by the time Sebastian found him in the wooded area of his neighbor's estate, the animal was half-conscious and whimpering in pain. The back leg was raw, the bone exposed, the chance for recovery nonexistent. Still, Sebastian could not accept the loss of his loyal companion, and he carried the animal, trap and all, to the barn, and contacted the physician. But it was too late; the dog died in his arms.

And now, the man looked as though he had seen death once again. His cravat lay on the floor, his shirt half-unbuttoned, wrinkled, and sticking out of his trousers. Sebastian Trent was known for his impeccable appearance and hair that was never mussed, not even a single strand out of place. But the man staring at Jason with bloodshot eyes and a frown on his face was as unrecognizable as the cravat on the floor.

"Good God, man, what happened?" Jason eyed the near-empty bottle on the desk. "I thought you detested drunkenness."

Sebastian lifted the bottle and drank straight from it, wiping his mouth with the back of his sleeve. "I do, but there are times when it fits the occasion."

Jason eased the bottle from Sebastian's hand and set it on the table beside him. "How about you leave off of that for now and tell me what has you in such a mess?" Though he had a good idea what or rather who was responsible for the man's current state of confusion, drunkenness, and disarray. She had a name, too, one he was well familiar with—Ariana Kendrick.

Sebastian let out a long sigh, rested his head against the back of his chair, and closed his eyes. "The woman I love is not—" he paused, sighed again "—the woman I love."

"What nonsense is that?" So, she had told him the truth. Had she admitted everything, or just those parts that would make the whole situation more palatable for all parties concerned? Did Sebastian know the names of *all* parties concerned or had she conveniently left a few from her recollection? Like the fact that he was William's father? If she had admitted this truth, would his friend not have lunged at him, tried to land a punch or two? Perhaps she had not divulged the name of William's father. She might have said she was a widow or engaged when the man met his demise, through accident or otherwise. *Damn*, but he could not even venture to guess the woman's actions, much less her motives, and this proved most irritating.

"Ana is not Ana," Sebastian said, his voice slurring just so. "She is Ariana." He hiccoughed and repeated, "Ariana."

"I see. What a beautiful name."

Sebastian opened his eyes a fraction. "A beautiful name for a beautiful woman. Do you know she fabricated the widow's tale? She is not a widow at all. Am I such a fool to be duped by a beautiful woman in need? What is wrong with me?"

"You are an honorable man who believed the woman and her son needed help. No one could fault you for coming to their rescue." Jason clutched the arms of the chair and wished this meeting were over.

"But why am I always trying to rescue people? Why do I have this need to do so?" He raked a hand through his hair, making it stick straight up. "What is lacking in me? I could have my pick of women from here to the King's court and yet I choose the unavailable ones who do not necessarily want me to rescue them." He let out a cold, hollow laugh. "Maybe they are waiting for someone else to rescue them."

Jason grabbed the bottle of whisky and took a healthy swig. "Tell me the story. All of it." Before he left this room, he vowed his friend would know the whole truth, not just the convenient parts.

"If I've got to tell the tale, I'll need a bit of help." He held out a hand for the bottle and tossed back a good amount with nary a cough or sputter, not what one would expect of a person not unaccustomed to the drink.

Perhaps Sebastian had a greater familiarity with the stuff than he cared to admit. The drink did make the man spill all manner of interesting tidbits concerning Ariana with no reservation or concern for propriety. Jason rather liked this side of his friend and hoped to see more of it, minus the women problems. Complications involving a woman put a damper on a party every time. All was well, until Sebastian began to recount the first time he kissed Ariana.

"We sat in the drawing room, close enough for me to breathe her lavender scent. Ah, such a heady fragrance. Have you ever noticed how it fills your senses until you are smothered with it? If you took your last breath that very moment, it would be enough." He sighed. "I knew I loved her before our first kiss. But after that first kiss, when I looked into those blue eyes, so shiny, so mesmerizing, and tasted those lips—"

"Enough!"

"What?" Sebastian squinted at him. "What did I say?"

"What did you say? Do I need to tell you it is quite improper to regale the details of your physical association with a woman you are courting?"

Sebastian scratched his jaw, considered this. "But you asked why I was in a state and this is part of the story."

"Leave that part out. I will permit my imagination to fill in the blanks." Of course, at the moment, his imagination was painting bold and lust-filled pictures of his best friend and his ex-lover in compromising positions involving all manner of body parts, minus clothing. Had Ariana lain with Sebastian? Good God, he prayed she had not.

"My imagination has filled in the blanks many times, in hopes that one day I would match my imagination with the truth. Sadly, I shall never learn how close or far apart they are."

So, he had not slept with Ariana! It should not matter to Jason, but he was not fool enough to pretend it did not. From the moment he saw her enter Sebastian's drawing room, he had been consumed with her as though nine years and a monster of a father did not stand between them.

"Sebastian? Did Ariana tell you anything about William's father?"

He shook his head. "Nothing of consequence." Pause. "She did say something about too much hurt and years of lies separating them, but that could be half the men of the ton, wouldn't you say?"

"But it is not," Jason said quietly. "It is only one man."

Sebastian hefted the bottle and took a drink. "Lucky bastard."

"I believe I know who William's father is."

"You do? Who is it and how would you know?"

"I would know because I believe it is…me."

"You? How? I mean…what the hell?"

"I am almost certain I am William's father, though Ariana denies it. We were together one summer before I returned to Oxford. I never knew she was carrying my child and her father made the mistake of contacting mine."

"Good God." Sebastian dragged his hands over his face. "You and Ariana."

"I'm sorry. When you told me about her, I had no idea it was Ariana."

"I do not know if I want to shake your hand or challenge you to a duel."

Jason met his gaze, held it. "I would venture to say a bit of both."

"She was never mine, no matter how much I wished it. That is the bold truth and one I must accept. Despite my bruised heart and wounded ego, we must work together to ensure the safety of William and Ana—I mean, Ariana. Once we know they are in no danger of being snatched in the night, I believe I will take an extended trip where no one has ever heard of Sebastian Trent."

"I believe that is an excellent plan, and well deserved." Jason extended a hand. "Thank you."

Sebastian nodded and shook Jason's hand, proving once again, the man was an honorable and most trustworthy gentleman.

***

My Dearest Jason:

I miss you so! The days are long since you are not here to brighten them with your smile. I should be most angry with you for leaving me before the Autumn Ball, but I shall endeavor to forgive you as the purpose of your trip to England was for me.

I do hope you have spoken with your brother and sister and informed them of your intent to return to America and remain here. Of course, I know you have not spoken the words to me yet and it is unladylike to presume, but I am most anxious to hear those words! I imagine them falling from your lips each night as I drift to sleep. Oh, but how I long to hear them.

Soon, my love? Please do make it soon. There is much to plan and I am most eager to begin.

All of my love,
Melanie

Jason reread the letter three times. It did not take someone as skilled in analyzing as Alexander Bishop, to know that Melanie Fontaine expected him to offer for her. He had never come out and said he planned to do so, but he certainly had implied it. More than once. Of course, she had been the one who encouraged him, even hinted she would be amenable to such an arrangement, long before the thought entered his head.

He should have spoken to Holt and Julia about his plans to remain in America the day he arrived. Why had he hesitated? Could it be that the idea of marrying Melanie was more pleasing than actually marrying her? And if he were being truthful with himself, why not admit that once he saw Ariana, despite her fabrications and engagement to his best friend, he had not thought about offering for Melanie Fontaine. In fact, he had not thought of her at all.

Now what did that say about the situation? He stared at the words, *All my love*, until they blurred. Then he crumpled the letter and tossed it into the fire, watching whatever affection he once felt for Melanie smolder and turn to embers.

***

Jason had spent the last few hours reviewing Holt's plans for the new ship he would build next spring. Not that his brother required his help or approval; since merging

Langford and Seacrest Shipping, the business had not only thrived, but burst with expansion. Holt had the best business partner possible in his wife. Sophie knew the shipping business, knew what was required to build a sturdy and reputable vessel, as well as the skills necessary to facilitate growth.

Holt and Sophie were indeed the perfect match, in business and in their personal lives. Jason supposed when one had the right partner, anything was possible. However, his brother and sister-in-law had not always been so perfect for one another. In fact, there had been a time when...

"Jason?" Holt poked his head in the library and said, "I have come to say good-bye. Sophie and Julia are packing up the children and have somehow convinced me to spend a few days in the city. Not to my liking, but I suppose compromise is key."

"I suppose so." What did he know about compromise? The only woman he'd ever cared about had not been interested in sharing anything with him, not even a compromise.

"At least one of us will enjoy the quiet." Holt lifted a hand in farewell and closed the door.

Jason rose from the desk and made his way to the sideboard. Too much quiet invited thoughts he would rather not acknowledge and a whisky or two might blur those thoughts.

"Hello, Jason."

That voice caught him by surprise. He swung around, came face to face with Ariana. "Ariana?"

"I know I should not have come unannounced, but I had to speak with you." Her eyes shimmered with tears that spoke of pain and sadness. "We have both hurt Sebastian, even though it was not our intent, and we had no possible way of knowing his connection with us. I believe we have broken his heart."

"Sadly, I believe you are correct." Jason downed his drink and set the glass on the edge of the desk. "You know he would still marry you."

"I do, but how could I possibly accept?"

He ran a hand through his hair, forced himself not to go to her for fear he would do something idiotic, like touch her. "More than one marriage has been of convenience and not love."

"But how sad." Her words fell out in a whisper. "How pathetically tragic, especially when one has seen glimpses of…" She caught herself, stopped, and cleared her throat.

Damn, but his body refused to listen to his head as he moved toward her. "Seen glimpses of what?" He cupped her chin with his fingers and met her gaze. "Tell me."

She blinked, blinked again. "Of how things could be," she whispered, "when there is love."

He trailed a hand along her cheek, traced her jaw. "I told him about us. And William. Part of me wanted to protect him from that, and yet another part knew that once I spoke the words, he would understand he could never be with you—" he paused, sucked in a breath as the truth settled in his brain "—because we belong together. No matter how much we fight it, no matter how much circumstance and fate try to prevent it, you and I, Ariana Kendrick, belong together."

She took his hand, brought it to her lips, kissed each finger. "I have dreamed this a thousand times, knowing it would most likely remain a dream."

He held her gaze, willed her to believe in him, believe in them. "Dreams can come true, if we want them enough."

She squeezed his hand. "I am afraid to want this."

"No." He brushed a curl from her forehead, planted a kiss on her mouth. "Do not be afraid. I will protect you," he murmured against her lips. "Always."

"Jason," she breathed, seconds before she buried her fingers in his hair and pressed her body against his.

He deepened the kiss, devouring her with his mouth as he lifted her gown, ran a hand over the softness of her thigh. Oh, but he wanted her. Badly. Deeply, with such need if he were not careful, their lovemaking would be over before it started. He was no longer the young, eager boy who let pleasure rule over skill and technique. No woman left his bed unsatisfied, or without hopes of entering it again as soon as possible. Jason wanted this union to be perfect, because this was Ariana. The woman he had never forgotten. The woman he loved. He must go slowly…think of her…ignore the passion thrumming inside him…

"Love me, Jason." She nipped his neck, ran her tongue along his jaw. "Love me."

To hell with patience and ignoring passion. He worked his fingers inside her pantaloons, stroked her *there*…She cupped him, touched his hardness through his breeches, flipped open one button, then the next, creating an exquisite agony that was a mixture of pleasure and pain. She had always known how to bring him to the very edge. He eased her pantaloons down her hips, buried a finger deep inside her heat. "I have missed you. There has never been anyone like you."

She sucked the tender spot on his neck, let out a low rumble of laughter, and yanked down his breeches, her fingers circling his sex. "Oh, Jason, there has never been anyone *but* you."

Her words pulsed through him in a rage of heat and desire. "If you do not slow down, and ease the torments and teasing, I shall not be responsible for my actions." He nipped her neck, laughed. "And the actions will be hard and deep and long. Quite long."

Ariana dropped her hands to her sides and eased away. "Indeed?" A smile crept upon her lips as she leaned against his desk, lifted her gown to the top of her thighs, and planted her slippered feet apart. "I would know how hard, how deep, and how long." The smile spread as she lifted the gown higher.

"Ariana," he groaned.

She hoisted herself onto the edge of the desk, leaned back, and inched her legs apart. The hem of her gown covered her woman's heat, but just barely. That proved as seductive as if she had stripped and stood before him, gloriously naked. That vision provided its own form of tantalizing possibilities, one he would enjoy soon enough. "Yes?"

"I am in pain," he said.

She slid her gaze to his open breeches, ran her tongue along her lower lip. "I do not wish to see you in pain." Those damnable legs eased open further. "May I help?"

His sex bobbed and jumped with desire. "Oh, yes, I do believe you can help." He scooped her off the desk and impaled her with a groan. Ariana clung to him, legs wrapped around his waist; breasts pressed against his chest as she rode him, gently at first, then harder, faster, with more urgency, until she arched against him and cried out her release. Jason followed, thrusting deeply, her name on his lips as he exploded in a burst of passion and spilled himself inside her.

When their sighs faded and their breathing evened, the room filled with the sound of the ticking clock and the crackling fire. They lay on the Aubusson rug, covered with a large afghan. Jason stroked Ariana's hair, his fingers sifting through her curls. If he had the rest of his life to spend with her, it would not be enough. Her eyes were closed, her breath faint, her lips partly open. Was she simply resting or was she already regretting what they had done? Jason hoped to God it was not the latter, for he certainly did not regret it, and wished for more. Much more. A lifetime more.

"Jason?" Ariana's eyes were open, her fingers stroking his cheek. "Why such a stern look?"

This was no time to hide his feelings, not when the woman he wanted to spend his life with lay beside him. "I love you," he blurted out. "Marry me. As soon as possible."

"Are you trying to be honorable to make up for what happened nine years ago?"

He did not miss the tightness in her voice. "I would give a limb to have married you back then and shared a life with you, but it was not meant to be." He grasped her hand, brought it to his lips, and kissed it. "Now we have a second chance, a real one, and I want it. With you."

"I love you, Jason Langford. You own my heart." She leaned forward, kissed his forehead, his nose, his mouth. "Always." Another kiss, this one on his neck. "Forever. And beyond."

Jason laughed and lay on his back, pulling her on top of him. "We must tell William the truth about us." When she nodded, he said, "He should know you are his true mother and I am his father. We have much explaining to do, and he will not be the only one with questions."

"I daresay everyone will have an overabundance of questions, including the staff." She shook her head and sighed. "I have tried very hard to lead an unremarkable life these past years so as not to draw attention, but once the gossipmongers learn of this, we shall be the topic of every conversation, great and small."

"Yes." And then, "Do you care?"

Her blue eyes sparkled. "Not if it means being with you." She kissed his mouth, eased onto his sex, and sighed. "I shall be perfectly happy to remain like this forever."

He liked the sound of that. Forever.

Chapter 6

Jason's hope for a second chance with Ariana ended the next afternoon when Jaffe informed him he had a visitor. He was fairly certain this visitor would be Sebastian Trent or Alexander Bishop, but he was wrong. When a vision of royal blue and lace swirled into the drawing room, there were no words to express his shock. There were no words at all.

"Jason!" Melanie Fontaine descended upon him in a mix of laughter and lilac, throwing her hands about his neck and reaching on tiptoe for a kiss. Not the kind of kiss he had shared with Ariana last evening, but a peck, three of them in rapid succession. He forced a smile and worked a calm into his voice. "Melanie. What a surprise."

"I hope you do not mind. Douglas said I was being overly bold, but what does my cousin know of such things? If it does not contain numbers, he is lost."

Melanie should have listened to Douglas Fontaine, for in this case, the man was spot on. Overly bold was a true understatement. One did not travel the ocean to "surprise" someone, unless it was a betrothed or a spouse, and often, not even then.

If it were Ariana, Jason would wish her to travel three continents and five oceans to see him and he would do the same for her. But then he loved her. He merely felt affection for Melanie, and while he had come close to offering for her because he believed real love did not exist, he knew differently now. Everything had changed the moment he spotted Ariana.

"Jason? Why such a frown?" Her own mouth pulled into a frown. "Is something wrong?" Pause. "Was my cousin right? Should I not have come to you?"

What could he say?

"Jason? Do you no longer care for me? I thought your purpose for this visit was because of me."

"I do care for you, Melanie." *But I love Ariana.*

She blew out a long breath. "Thank goodness." Her smile turned bright, spilled over him. "Mama and I have begun shopping for gowns and such—" she slid him a look and batted her eyes at him "—for when the time comes. Oh, now do not look at me as though you just tasted a lemon tart. Preparation and planning are essential, and that is all we are doing." When his frown deepened, she batted her lashes again and added, "Truly."

He was supposed to meet Ariana this afternoon so they could tell William they were his parents. It was not a task he looked forward to, but he hoped that in time the boy would accept him, maybe one day call him Father. This relationship business was foreign to him, and other than what he shared with Ariana years ago, only his family had been permitted access to his real feelings. But now he would be a husband and a father, to William and, God willing, other children. There was much to think about, but before he could begin planning a future with Ariana and William, he had to pay a visit to Sebastian, and then his family and the Bishops, though Jason would not be surprised if Alexander Bishop had not surmised the truth already.

"Ellswood is indeed a grand home." Melanie swept a gaze around the room, eyeing the draperies, the paintings, the vases on the mantel. "I could learn to live here, of that I am certain."

"This is my brother's home," Jason said, a bit annoyed with the proprietary air of her comment. He had not asked her to live here, had not even offered for her, and yet Melanie treated him *and* their relationship as though he had.

Her cousin, Douglas, had once told him that Melanie did not like disappointment, especially her own, and had yet to learn when to back out of a losing proposition. Well, she was about to lose in the "gain a proposal from Jason Langford" area, and he wished he did not have to be present when she did. Unfortunately, he would not only be present, he would be the one delivering the blow.

"Oh, Jason, of course it is your brother's home, but surely you shall have one that carries a magnificence of its own." Her eyes sparkled and her voice turned soft and persuasive. "Whether you have one here in England, or in America, it shall not matter." She tilted her head to one side, tapped her chin. "I had never considered life here, but there is much to be said for decorum and titles—" she slid him a glance and stroked his cheek "—and it appears the Langford name is indeed plump with both."

Jason forced a smile, wishing he were with Ariana right now and away from Melanie's calculations of titles and wealth. "The Langfords are indeed an interesting lot." Should he tell her of his father's cruelty and his mother's insanity? Perhaps he should toss in the fact that his mother murdered Sophie's mother when she learned the woman was having an affair with her husband. Melanie's head might turn a time or two when she spotted elegance in the form of wealth and title, but she would not like to learn of scandal and certainly not that the Langford name was rife with it.

"Interesting and exceptional." She kissed him softly on the mouth, buried her head against his chest, and sighed. "I have missed you so. I never wish to be parted from you again."

"Melanie." He could not let her go on and on about missing him and wishing to be with him, not when his heart was full of another woman—the only woman he had ever loved. Once she had food in her belly and a bit of rest, Jason would tell Melanie there would be no offer of marriage.

"Do not speak now, my love." She snuggled against him. "Let me breathe your scent, let me find peace in your words, and your strength."

Jason permitted her this final moment, his arms slung loosely around her back, his brain rehearsing the words he would say soon enough. *I apologize if I have misled you, but I cannot marry you.*

The muffled gasp from across the room startled him. Ariana stood in the doorway, her face a mix of shock and grief, so deep it pierced his soul.

And then she was gone.

***

"Well, I daresay you have made a mess of things. That was not well done."

Jason scowled at Alexander Bishop. That was one thing about the man; he did so love to state the obvious. "I know I've mucked it up with Ariana, but how was I to know Melanie would sail across an ocean on a whim?"

Bishop toyed with a paperweight, set it down, and studied Jason from the other side of his desk. "I could ask why Melanie exists in the first place or why you did not terminate the 'relationship' before you picked up with Ariana. You cannot proclaim true love and everlasting devotion to one woman when you have another waiting for you."

"I know that, damn it." Jason raked both hands through his hair and pinched the bridge of his nose.

"Your first mistake was promising yourself to another and then proposing to Ariana."

"I did not promise myself to Melanie." He paused,

scratched his jaw. "She interpreted it as such."

"And you did nothing to encourage her interpretation or refute it?"

Jason shrugged. "It did not seem to matter at the time. I believed Ariana dead and did not think true love existed."

Bishop cocked a dark brow. "And now you believe it does?"

"Now I know it does." Such simple words, locked into such deep feelings.

"It would appear you have a predicament, one that requires assistance if you are to find a way out of the hole you've dug."

"And you have a plan?" Jason had gone after Ariana and tried to explain that what she had seen was not really what it looked like. But what was that? A woman embracing him, head on his shoulder, murmuring words of love? He might not have wanted to hear the words or feel Melanie Fontaine's supple body against his, but it *had* been an embrace and the words had been love-filled. Ariana would hear none of it. She had slapped his face, cursed him to hell, and called him a liar and a cheat. And he had felt like all of those.

"Of course I have a plan." Bishop poured them both a whisky and handed one to him. "I always have a plan, though this is a bit out of my area." He took a healthy swallow and sighed. "Relationships are not my strong suit. I would sooner bathe in mud than dissect one, but Francie has asked for my help."

The man obviously was not comfortable with his wife's request, yet here he was, engaging in a task he abhorred. "Do you always agree to your wife's demands?"

Bishop seemed honestly perplexed. "They are not demands, they are requests. There is a marked difference.

Were my wife demanding I do as she asked, I imagine I would balk and refuse. But a request, well, that is something else altogether, and when asked with the sweetness of a strawberry, how could I refuse?"

"Right." Listening to Alexander Bishop compare his wife's words to strawberries was an oddity indeed, but Jason would listen to him compare the woman's animals to the sweetest-smelling fragrance on this earth, if he could help make things right with Ariana.

"You know she hates you at the moment," Bishop said, eyeing him over his glass of whisky. "Putrid, foul, stab-you-in-the eye hatred."

"I get the picture." He did not have to elaborate; it had all been on her face when she spotted him with Melanie.

"Francie brought her to me seconds after she returned from Ellswood and asked for my help. The woman could not stop crying." He shook his head. "I cannot abide tears, but there she was, pouring buckets, with me at her side, my handkerchief at the ready. But those tears would have required five handkerchiefs, or maybe a sheet to sop them up. Ariana told us the sad tale of your previous relationship and—" he paused, cleared his throat "—union, as well as the truth about William, which, of course, did not come as a surprise to me."

"Damn it, Bishop, have you never messed up with Francie? Not even once?"

That silver gaze narrowed, the lips flattened. "Oh, yes, I did. I almost lost her because of my arrogance and inability to admit I needed her. Did you know Sebastian had an eye on her? He would have made an excellent husband, and yet, I could not give her up, nor could I admit I wanted her for myself." He cleared his throat and straightened his cravat, signaling the end to a story Jason wished to know more about. "Now to our plan. Sebastian and I will speak with Miss Fontaine and make her aware that you are off the marriage mart. I have no doubt we can be most persuasive."

"Sebastian? He has agreed to this?"

"It was his idea. We will take care of Miss Fontaine and provide her with a few options we believe she will agree to, but it is up to you to set things right with Ariana." He downed the rest of his drink and smiled, a real smile, and added, "I have given you a good amount of leverage. Just do not muck things up again and there shall be a wedding before spring."

Jason nodded. "Thank you. Very much."

"There is one more thing. I planned to tell you earlier, before this present emergency arose. Sebastian and I have located the mysterious earl. Once Ariana gave us his name, the rest was basic deduction. His name is Reginald Hawthorne, the earl of Nightingale, a man known for his women and his risk taking. It is said he made enormous amounts of money in the stock market and then made loans to his less fortunate friends at very high interest rates. When they defaulted, he took their properties—" he paused, rubbed his jaw, and said in a quiet voice "—or other forms of payment, often a young daughter or two."

"Bastard."

"He never touched Ariana, but then he was rarely in residence. She and William formed an odd bond of sorts with Lady Nightingale, and the woman intended to provide for them should something happen to her. Unfortunately, her husband had other plans, and they involved Ariana sharing his bed."

Jason clenched and unclenched his fists as he listened to Bishop recall the story with little emotion on his face and even less in his voice. He might well have been talking about the selection of a cravat or pair of boots. But when next the man spoke, he left no doubt that he would see Reginald Hawthorne pay dearly for his threats to Ariana. Not only that, but the man would pay for engaging in unsavory business with a man like Edward Langford where lives were disregarded. "Hawthorne is heavily invested in certain stocks, and it would be disastrous for him if those stocks suffered huge losses." His silver gaze narrowed. "I shall see that it happens and when he is desperate and sinking, I shall offer him a rope at which time he may save himself by never mentioning Ariana or William's name again. Or, should he choose to ignore the offer, I shall let him hang."

***

Melanie Fontaine had not finished stirring the sugar cube in her tea before Alexander made a significant discovery. The woman was not necessarily in love with Jason Langford, but she *was* enamored with marrying a titled gentleman. Langford may have simply been the best of the lot, but the woman was in England now, where titles and wealth were more than abundant. While Langford was a decent chap with a ready smile and casual manner, he was the *second* son of an earl, not the prized first son.

Damn, why could more women not be like Francie? She had no need for titles and treated their cook with the same generosity she showed dinner guests. That was just Francie's way and he would not want to change her, though at times he wished her a bit more interested in decorum. If this baby were a girl, he would bet his latest stock pick that his wife would have the child in her brothers' breeches before she could walk.

"I must admit, I am a bit perplexed by your invitation." Melanie Fontaine glanced at Alexander and then Sebastian.

"I have suffered a horrible shock and I do not believe I shall recover for some time. However, politeness and a certain curiosity dictated I accept your invitation."

"We understand, and we are most grateful," Alexander said. She was referring to the "shock" of learning Jason loved another woman, and worse, that there would be no proposal. He sipped his tea and waited for Sebastian to say something. The man was a signature of decorum, but at present, he sat with his arms folded over his chest, a frown on his face, gaze narrowed—as though he were not impressed with their guest or her "politeness."

"Jason is in love with Ariana Kendrick and whatever relationship he may or may not have shared with you is over." Sebastian's tone said he did not care if he offended the woman. Strange that. Alexander had not thought the man capable of rudeness, but there it was, cold words spread out on a blanket of irritation.

Melanie Fontaine's creamy complexion turned bright pink, her tiny nostrils flaring as she stirred her tea faster and spilled out a rebuttal. "You would have me tossed aside like so much rubbish? I have spent months in Jason Langford's company, traveled an ocean to be with him, and now I am simply to step aside?"

"Are you sorry that Jason has chosen another, or that you have lost so much time husband hunting the wrong man?"

Oh, but Sebastian was brutal in his commentary. Alexander cleared his throat and slid a glance at his friend. What had gotten into the man? He sounded more like Alexander than...well, than Alexander did. Perhaps he had grown tired of being the target of women who hunted men for their wealth and titles and while he might not defend himself, he was not going to let this happen to Jason.

Melanie Fontaine gasped. "I care for Jason. Deeply." She

sniffed, pulled out a handkerchief, and dabbed her eyes. "I love him," she whispered.

"Indeed." Sebastian leaned toward her, an action that caused her to square her shoulders. "Your love for him is irrelevant. Jason believed Ariana was dead, thanks to the manipulations of a ruthless father."

"Yes," Alexander interjected before Sebastian hurled more barbs at the woman about the irrelevance of her love. "Jason's father had no qualms exercising power over others, to the point of destroying lives, even those of his children." He sighed, paused long enough for what he hoped would elicit sympathy for Jason and Ariana's tale, and finished with, "Imagine finding the woman you believed dead was not dead at all, and your father had orchestrated her disappearance?"

"Could have been a tragic opera," Sebastian added, his smile tight.

"I believe it is an opera," Alexander added. "I must ask my wife, as I defer to her on all such matters."

"And what of me?" Melanie Fontaine asked. "Am I to suffer the humiliation of returning to America without a proposal? People will say I am forward and that I had no business making presumptions that Jason would offer for me."

"Yes, they probably will say all of those things and more." Sebastian stared at her. "And they will be right. However, would you wish to wed a man who loves another? Who will always love another?"

Melanie Fontaine picked at a spot on her gown and remained silent.

"Of course not," Alexander said when the woman did not answer. "What if you were offered an introduction to the most eligible bachelors of the ton? Men with titles and money who are looking for a suitable wife? Would you agree to such an arrangement?"

"I—"

"Of course she would." Sebastian's scowl said he did not particularly enjoy this thought.

"You are the daughter of a baron, are you not?" Alexander asked.

She nodded. "Yes, I am." She tilted her chin in the air and shifted her body so she could ignore Sebastian, who was not going to be ignored if the frown he wore were an indication.

"Well then. I believe this could prove interesting. Why not venture to London, attend a few soirees and balls, and see what happens? I have a townhouse there and it will be at your disposal."

The shine in her hazel eyes told him she liked the sound of that, very much. "I did not bring proper attire to travel among the ton and attend soirees and balls." She sighed and did her best to appear distraught, but Alexander saw it for what it was—a ploy to obtain a new ball gown or three— and he bet Sebastian did, too.

"Gowns are the least of your concern," Sebastian said. "It is the introduction that will matter, and it must come from someone with influence, wealth, and a title."

"Yes, that is exactly correct," Alexander said, feigning innocence. He knew the person for the job and the man sat in this room.

"But who?" Melanie Fontaine asked in a breath of anticipation mixed with excitement. "Do you know of someone?"

"Of course he does," Sebastian said with a tight smile. "Me."

After Sebastian's announcement, Alexander swore the

woman was close to refusing an offer that moments ago had her gasping with excitement. But after another cup of tea and a frown or two, she grudgingly accepted, hinting more than once she would rather a different member of the ton make the introduction—anyone but Sebastian Trent.

"Thank God the woman is gone," Sebastian said when Melanie Fontaine bid her good-byes. She and her chaperone would leave immediately for London and await Sebastian's arrival, at which time he would introduce her to London and the eligible bachelors of the ton.

Alexander hid a smile. "I do believe I feel a headache coming on and it has a name." He paused and the smile slipped out. "Miss Melanie Fontaine."

Sebastian laughed. "Indeed. How did Jason tolerate her?" He shook his head, laughed again.

"I commend you for what you are doing. I'm certain you would prefer other forms of agony than escorting Miss Fontaine about London and listening to her expound on titles and wealth."

"Despite what has happened with Ariana, Jason is my friend." He glanced at Alexander, narrowed his gaze on him. "I could say the same of you. Why did you help him? I would not have thought you would get involved in such a situation, for it smacks of emotion and I did not think you could abide those."

Alexander shrugged. "Showing them to anyone but my wife is not my preference, but what choice did I have? Jason is my friend."

Chapter 7

Melanie was gone, whisked away with her chaperone in a carriage bearing the Montrose crest. Very interesting. More interesting was the note delivered an hour ago.

Jason:

Miss Fontaine and her chaperone are traveling to London for an extended stay. Sebastian has agreed to show Miss Fontaine the sights and whatnot. She is quite eager to meet England's most eligible bachelors. I am certain you are delighted that you are no longer among that group, and Miss Fontaine understands and accept that fact.

Best to Ariana.

Alexander Bishop

He would not have guessed Alexander would become so involved in a personal situation like this. Was his wife behind it? Francie Bishop was usually at the bottom of a relationship issue, especially in regard to matchmaking. Perhaps he owed the woman a visit to thank her for persuading her husband to act on Jason's behalf and coax Melanie from Ellswood. What of Sebastian? Had he willingly agreed to escort her about London? Such actions were the mark of true friendship and Jason would remain indebted to him. And whether Francie Bishop was behind her husband's actions or not, Jason realized he had a friend in the man, even if Bishop never admitted it.

Where did Melanie's departure leave him and Ariana? His father had fabricated a betrothal when there had been none, and Melanie's arrival hinted at one that while not formal, had indeed been forthcoming. Would Ariana ever forgive him? Permit him another chance to make things right? If she would find it in her heart to consider forgiveness, he would spend his life earning back her trust and perhaps one day, her love.

"Excuse me, sir, but you have a visitor."

Jason glanced up from the notes he should have been reviewing in regard to Holt's proposed ship and realized he had not read the first word. "Who is it, Jaffe? I really am not in the mood for more visitors."

The butler coughed and cleared his throat. "It is Miss Kendrick, sir."

Ariana was here? "Oh." Jason pushed back his chair and stood. "Show her in at once." Had she come to bid him farewell or, hope upon hope, offer him another chance? When Jaffe ushered her in, he could do no more than stare as she moved toward him, a hesitant smile upon her face.

"Hello, Jason."

He nodded, attempted to discern the reason behind her smile and when he could not, he said, "Hello, Ariana."

"I do hope I am not intruding—" she glanced at the papers strewn about his desk "—but I had need to speak with you as soon as possible."

"You are not intruding." *I would wish you at my side every day and every night, until I draw my last breath.*

"Thank you…I…have recently learned that…that you…" she faltered, looked away.

Why was she acting so skittish? "Ariana? What is it?"

She dragged her gaze to his and blurted out, "That you provided for my family."

Where had she heard that? Jason forced himself to remain calm, his expression blank. *Damn, but who had told her such a thing, and why?* "Go on."

"So, you do not deny it?" Her eyes grew bright, her

voice soft.

"What is it I am to have done?" It took great effort to force a smile, but he managed. "Moreover, who said I have done it?"

"I trust the man who told me; he is not only honest but honorable. He said you paid for my parents' burials, and found employment for my sisters in fine homes." Those blue eyes filled with tears. "Hope as a lady's maid, and Rachel as a cook's assistant."

Jason only knew of two men who might have acquired such information: Sebastian Trent and Alexander Bishop.

"Jason?" Her voice spilled over him, warm as honey and equally sweet. "Alexander Bishop told me."

Damn that man. Jason rather thought he liked the man better when he was taciturn and sullen. He was beginning to think Bishop was more of a busybody than his wife! "He had no right to divulge such information, whether it be true or not."

Ariana moved toward him and said in the softest of voices, "Alexander Bishop had every right to tell me. You are his friend and he wished me to know. I did not trust you and judged you harshly, but you helped my family." She brought his hands to her lips, kissed his knuckles. "I shall never be able to repay you for what you have done."

"I should have done more; I wish I had, but I did not understand their reduced circumstances until your mother's death."

"But why did you help them? You had no idea what your father had done."

"I helped them because of you." He unclasped her hands, stroked her cheek. "Surely you must know that." The tears started then, trickling down her cheeks to her chin. Jason brushed them away and murmured, "Don't cry."

She sniffed, sniffed again. "How I would love to see my sisters. I wonder if I would recognize them."

He smiled and stroked her cheek. "You would recognize them. Rachel has your eyes, and Hope has your hair, though I am not certain if one or both sisters share your temperament."

"Will you take me to visit them?"

He eased away so he could see her face. "Exactly what did Alexander tell you about them?" The puzzled look on her face told him the man had not relayed a key factor in the tale—the location of their employer.

"He told me they worked in a fine house." She paused, her brows pinched together, and added, "I believe it was the home of an earl, but I cannot say for certain."

He nodded. "Yes, it is an earl, his wife, and their four daughters." He held her gaze. "In America. Richmond, Virginia."

"America?" she whispered.

Jason could not tell if she was pleased or furious, but either way he wanted to tell her why he had decided on a country an ocean away. "America has given them a fresh start. They work in the house of a friend of mine, and they are happy. I hear Hope has a young suitor who is a valet, and Rachel has many suitors." When Ariana continued to stare at him, he said, "I will take you to America, and ask nothing of you in return. However, if you can find it in your heart to forgive me and perhaps one day open your heart to me again, I would ask you to be my wife, and from this moment on, I will strive to bring joy to your life, and to William's." His voice cracked as he continued, "And all of the children who come after him."

"Jason." Her eyes shimmered and when she spoke, the love in her voice covered him. "I would be honored to be your wife—" her lips pulled into a wide smile filled with promise "—as soon as possible. I love you. I think I have never stopped loving you."

"My heart is filled with you, Ariana. Only you."

"We must tell William," she said. "I want him to know he has a mother and a father who love him, and aunts and uncles, like a real family."

"Yes." He smiled down at her. "Like a real family."

They were interrupted from further talk of America and families by a knock on the door. Jaffe entered and said, "Excuse me, sir, you have a visitor."

"Blast, can you not see I am busy?" And if the damn man would leave him alone, he might get busier with the undressing of his future wife.

"I apologize, sir, but he will not go away."

Jason sighed and turned to Ariana who nodded. "Very well. But return in two minutes to give him the boot." He flashed a smile at Ariana and said, "I have business to attend to." *Oh, yes, business indeed...the business of kissing, touching, and making love to the woman who owned his heart...*

"William?" Ariana rushed to her son, worry covering her face. "What is wrong? Why are you here?"

The boy cast a quick glance at Jason, then at his mother. "I know you have always told me it is impolite to eavesdrop and only bad comes of it." He pulled his face into a horrible frown, as though he were in agony, and said, "I should have listened, but I wanted to know about all of the secrets floating about. First, you are to marry Mr. Trent, but once Mr. Langford arrives, it appears you like him better." His voice dipped, filled with confusion. "I heard Mr. and Mrs. Bishop talking about it. Mr. Bishop said he and Mr. Trent were investigating my father, that he was not my real father at all, and the woman I thought was my mother was not. He said it was time to end the charade and place me with my real parents. What does that mean? Do you know who my real parents are?" Tears clogged his words, but he pushed on, "I want to know the truth." He turned to Jason, begged, "Please, do you know?"

God, but Jason hated to see the pain in the boy's eyes, the tragedy in his voice. "I do." He moved toward the boy, glanced at Ariana who nodded and said, "This is your mother. She gave birth to you but was blackmailed into permitting the earl and his wife to call you their child."

William hazarded a smile at his mother. "I have always pretended you were my real mother," he said. "Because I wished it so."

She threw her arms about him, hugged him close. "I love you, William. I have loved you since the moment you were born."

"And my father. Who is he?"

Jason met his son's innocent gaze and said, "I am your father."

"You, Mr. Langford?"

Jason nodded, pushed out the words. "I never knew you existed; I thought your mother dead."

"But you loved her then, and you love her still?"

The boy knew how to extract the truth. "Yes, I have always loved her."

He turned to Ariana. "And you love him, love him still?"

"Very much."

"So you will marry, and I will call you Mother, and I will not be play-acting." He slid a look at Jason. "And I will call you Father."

"If you so wish."

The boy nodded. "Yes, I would like that very much." He

held out a hand and Jason shook it, then pulled the boy into his arms for a hug.

"What would you say about traveling to America once your mother and I are married? I can show you what you have read about in books. I think you would enjoy it."

William's smile split open. "America? Truly?"

"Truly," Jason said.

William stood between Jason and Ariana, holding their hands between his, and said, "You must marry as soon as possible so we may begin our adventure in America." He grinned and squeezed Jason's hand. "I think you will make an excellent father, and I should wish for a brother and a sister, mayhap a dog or rabbit, too."

Ariana laughed and said, "Yes, William, yes to all of your requests."

Jason met her gaze over the top of their son's head and nodded. It had taken nine years to find his family, and he vowed it would take one hundred and nine to show them all the ways he loved them. He could not wait to begin.

Epilogue

"Alexander, you will never believe who paid me a visit."

Francie traced his left nipple, her naked body smothered with the scent of their lovemaking. He did not care to bring talk of visitors into their bed, but his wife would not be appeased until he inquired and she answered. He sighed, pulled her closer. The things a husband did to keep his wife happy…

"Who, my love?"

"Jason Langford." She lifted her head and smiled at him, her blue eyes bright. "I thought he did not care for me, but perhaps I was wrong."

"Perhaps you were," Alexander murmured. Of course, Langford liked Francie, who would not? Alexander would not tell her he had gently prompted the man to pay her a visit and make certain she knew he considered her a friend. Langford had not only done it, but had solicited Francie to help find a proper match for his sister, Julia. The man was too in love with his betrothed to realize no one *asks* Francie Bishop for matchmaking assistance, because the woman was past horrible at it. Oh well, love did make people do the strangest things…

"Alexander, I do believe you are becoming a matchmaker."

He stroked her hair, toyed with a plump red curl. "I do not think so, Francie. I am a businessman, not a matchmaker."

She laughed and laid her head on his chest, snuggling close. "You brought Jason and Ariana together, with the help of Sebastian. Poor man. I almost had that match, but how was I to know a long-lost love existed in Ariana's past?" She sighed. "Still, you are the one who found a way to bring them together and now look? There will be a wedding next month and then they will head to America where she will meet her sisters. Such a perfect ending. We could not ask for more."

"No, we could not, nor should we." Soon they would welcome their third child, and wagers were high this one would be a girl with fiery hair, blue eyes, and a wild streak like her mother. If that were the case, he had best store up sleep, for there would be none once such a child let out her first wail. Alexander closed his eyes, pictured a baby girl with her mother's looks and disposition, and smiled.

The End

Many thanks for choosing to spend your time reading *A Touch of Seduction*. I'm truly grateful. If you enjoyed it, please consider writing a review on the site where you purchased it. (Short ones are fine and equally welcome.) If you would like to read more Love & Betrayal...Regency Style works of mine, don't miss *The Redemption of Madeline Munrove,* Book One of The Model Wife series. (You'll meet Melanie Fontaine's American cousin, Douglas Fontaine, and learn how he plans to employ logic and reason to find a wife!) *The Redemption of Madeline Munrove* is available at most retailers: Kindle Nook iBooks Kobo

If you'd like to be notified of my new releases, please sign up at my website: *http://www.marycampisi.com*.

About the Author

Mary Campisi writes emotion-packed books about second chances. Whether contemporary romances, women's fiction, or Regency historicals, her books all center on belief in the beauty of that second chance.

Mary should have known she'd become a writer when at age thirteen she began changing the ending to all the books she read. It took several years and a number of jobs, including registered nurse, receptionist in a swanky hair salon, accounts payable clerk, and practice manager in an OB/GYN office, for her to rediscover writing. Enter a mouse-less computer, a floppy disk, and a dream large enough to fill a zip drive. The rest of the story lives on in every book she writes.

When she's not working on her craft or following the lives of five adult children, Mary's digging in the dirt with her flowers and herbs, cooking, reading, walking her rescue lab mix, Cooper, or on the perfect day, riding off into the sunset with her very own 'hero' husband on his Ultra Limited aka Harley.

Mary has published with Kensington, Carina Press, and The Wild Rose Press. She is currently working on her next A Family Affair book as the saga continues…

website: www.marycampisi.com
e-mail: mary@marycampisi.com
twitter: https://twitter.com/#!/MaryCampisi
blog: http://www.marycampisi.com/blog/
facebook: http://www.facebook.com/marycampisibooks

Other Books by Mary Campisi:

Contemporary Romance:

Truth in Lies Series
Book One: A Family Affair
Book Two: A Family Affair: Spring
Book Three: A Family Affair: Summer
Book Four: A Family Affair: Fall
Book Five: A Family Affair: Christmas
Book Six: A Family Affair: Winter ‾ (2015)
Book Seven: A Family Affair:..the saga continues (TBA)

That Second Chance Series
Book One: Pulling Home
Book Two: The Way They Were
Book Three: Simple Riches
Book Four: Paradise Found
Book Five: Not Your Everyday Housewife
Book Six: The Butterfly Garden

The Betrayed Trilogy
Book One: Pieces of You
Book Two: Secrets of You
Book Three: What's Left of Her: a novella
Boxed Set: The Betrayed Trilogy

Begin Again: Short stories from the heart
The Sweetest Deal

Regency Historical:

An Unlikely Husband Series

Book One - The Seduction of Sophie Seacrest

Book Two - A Taste of Seduction

Book Three - A Touch of Seduction, a novella

Book Four - A Scent of Seduction

The Model Wife Series

Book One: The Redemption of Madeline Munrove

Young Adult:

Pretending Normal